Mark Hebden is the author of numerous crime novels. He was a sailor, an airman, a journalist, a travel courier, a cartoonist and a history teacher. After turning to full-time writing, Hebden created a sequence of crime novels, inventing the well-known character of Inspector Pel.

BY THE SAME AUTHOR
ALL PUBLISHED BY HOUSE OF STRATUS

PeL
and the
Faceless
Corpse

MARK HEBDEN

HOUSE OF
STRATUS

Copyright © 1979, 2001 John Harris

This edition published in 2001 by House of Stratus, an imprint of Stratus Holdings plc, 24c Old Burlington Street, London, W1X 1RL, UK.

www.houseofstratus.com

Typeset, printed and bound by House of Stratus.

A catalogue record for this book is available from the British Library.

ISBN 1-84232-892-1

one

The pain in his chest was awful. It seemed to grind and twist below his heart, hot, searing and agonising, like an iron fist gripping his inside.

It was growing, becoming gradually worse, the pain sweeping under his breastbone in red-hot waves. He shifted miserably, aware that it was rapidly reaching the point when it would become unbearable.

Everything was black. He was wretched, alone and miserable. He put his hand out, reaching feebly, but there seemed to be chains round his limbs securing him to the bed. He seemed to be growing weaker, and as the pain came in increasing waves, he was certain he could never survive the night.

A drink would help. His lips were parched and his mouth dry. Could the wine he'd had to drink that evening have been poisoned?

Somewhere, miles away, he could hear a telephone ringing, noisy and repetitive. It beat on his brain like a cymbal, pounding at his senses, insistent, demanding, imperative. If only someone would answer it! He writhed on the bed, his limbs contorted. The cold in them spread. He could feel it reaching his chest. The pain grew worse. If this wasn't death, he felt, he didn't know what was...

'Merde alors!'

Jerking bolt upright in bed in a fury, Inspector Pel saw with disgust that the eiderdown had slipped off and he was freezing. His indigestion was giving him hell and the

1

telephone was yammering away. And, of course, because he was unmarried, there was nobody to answer it so he could sleep on in peace.

As he snatched up the telephone and barked at it, Sergeant Darcy answered. He was speaking from the office and he sounded so cheerful he might have been at a party.

'It's a murder, Patron,' he said. 'The Chief's given it to us.'

'Where is it?'

'In the woods at Butte-Avelan.'

'Where's that?'

'Orgny, Côte d'Or. Sergeant Massu, of the sub-station there reported it.'

'Who is it?'

'We don't know yet.' Darcy paused. 'I should put something warm on, Patron,' he warned. 'It's a cold night and Butte-Avelan's high ground.'

Probably as high as Mont Blanc, Pel thought bitterly, and covered with ice all year round.

Ringing off, he called Transport and asked to be picked up, then, because it had been bitterly cold for days, with nights of deep frosts with the ground like iron and the grass silver-white with hoar rime, he decided it would be wise to be on the safe side, and put on three sweaters and dug out a scarf. His blood was always thin at this time of the year, and the night's operations would probably bring him down with pneumonia. Since, like all Frenchmen, he had learned in minute detail at school every part of the body and its functions, Pel suffered from a severe case of a little knowledge being dangerous, and was always convinced he was on the verge either of a nervous breakdown or a complete collapse in his health. The fact that his slight frame was always able to go on when all his colleagues had fallen by the wayside with exhaustion never managed to convince him to the contrary and he spent most of his days in a gloomy fear that they were to be his last.

He didn't bother to shave. There'd be time for that later, he thought; the French, unlike the British, were too realistic to set much store by personal appearances when speed was essential. Thinking about speed, he wondered if he could delay long enough to make himself a cup of coffee – Hag, of course; decaffeinated, so it wouldn't harm him – but in the end he decided he hadn't time and settled for a glass of brandy. Only to warm him up, he tried to persuade himself, because, falling as it would on an empty stomach, he knew it would give him hell later.

Shuddering at the thought of going out in the middle of a November night – at six o'clock in the morning, it was as good as night – he heard his housekeeper, Madame Routy, give a little snuffling snore as he passed her door. He stared at it bitterly, wondering why he couldn't be like Maigret whose wife always got up when he was called out and had soup or coffee ready for him before he left.

Going downstairs, he poured himself a brandy, drank it quickly, and for safety popped a bismuth tablet into his mouth. Taking from his pocket a small device of rollers covered with rubber, he proceeded to fill it with tobacco from a packet marked 'Samson Halfzware Shag'. In his agonised efforts to cut down on his smoking, he'd taken to the desperate remedy of rolling his own, and during a recent visit to Holland on an enquiry had come back armed with Dutch tobacco and a British roller and cigarette papers.

Concentrating fiercely, he turned out a bent and wilting tube which he put in his mouth. As he applied a match, there was a shower of sparks and the cigarette vanished in a puff of smoke. Determined not to be beaten, he tried again but this time he put in too much tobacco and the effort of drawing the smoke down made his eyes bulge. Furious and frustrated at his lack of success, he was still trying when the car arrived.

It had been snowing and the city's famous coloured roofs were hidden and the trees were stark and black. Winter always laid bare the bones of a city and, like unhappiness, seemed to bite more in the streets than in the country. And this winter, Pel decided, seemed to have lasted all his life.

At the Hôtel de Police everybody was looking glum. The man at the enquiry desk was looking glum because he had a cold coming on and the draught from the door had fangs and claws in it. The sergeant was looking glum because he was just pinning up on the board a notice which had come from St Etienne further south. It asked for information on a gang of four men who had jumped from a car at Firmin three days before and filled the air with flying bullets to keep everybody's head down while they'd robbed a branch of Crédit Lyonnais. Two policemen who'd stopped their car on a lonely road near St Symphorien as they'd escaped had been shot to death and the gangsters had helped themselves to the dead men's .38s, probably because they were running out of ammunition for their own. The sergeant considered it something to be glum about when policemen's lives were regarded as possessing so little value.

Misset was sitting in the detective sergeants' room looking glum because, as he'd confided to Pel that day, his wife was expecting another baby and he knew he couldn't afford it, and that his work schedules would have to be adjusted so he could give her a bit of help. Krauss was looking glum because he was fat and due for retirement and didn't consider being turned out on a cold night one of the pleasanter aspects of a policeman's lot. He was already involved in the case of the Mysterious Chicken Stealer. Up near Orgny, where the murder had taken place, there had been cases of chickens disappearing and since some of them had belonged to a farmer friend of the Chief of Police, they'd had to look into them. Krauss had landed the job because he was the oldest and the slowest. Even Nosjean, who was young enough still to have a face like a choirboy, was looking glum, and Pel suspected he was having trouble with his girlfriend again. Nosjean had girl troubles as dogs had fleas.

Only Sergeant Daniel Darcy wasn't looking glum. He was in Pel's office, using the spare telephone, and as Pel entered, he smiled and lifted a hand in salute. He looked so pleased with himself, you could have assumed that one of his chief joys in life was being dragged out in the early hours of a November morning. He looked so happy, Pel hated him.

As he put down the telephone, Pel opened his mouth to ask whether Lab, Fingerprints, Photography and all the other odds and ends had been informed, but Darcy, who was nothing if not efficient, was too quick for him and informed him that they had.

Pel grunted. After all, he thought, why shouldn't *they* suffer too? 'They got me out of my bed –' he began.

'They got me out of *someone else's* bed,' Darcy said.

Pel frowned. 'You're always in someone else's bed.'

'Well, these lonely women –' Darcy smiled. 'That's what *you* need, Patron. A woman. To love and cherish you. You'd feel fulfilled. Life would change. The day would be full of laughter and song.'

Pel glared. 'Tell me the worst,' he said.

'Nothing to worry about,' Darcy said. 'Everything's under control.'

'With bodies being found all over Burgundy?' Pel's eyebrows shot up to the sparse hair he flattened to his skull. 'Sometimes, I think you have a curious idea of what's normal.'

'These days,' Darcy said cheerfully, 'with terrorists, kidnappers and so on everywhere, it wouldn't be normal if there *weren't* bodies lying about.'

Pel digested this, trying in vain to find a scathing reply. 'What do we know?' he growled.

'Male,' Darcy said. 'Aged fifty to sixty. Grey-haired, running to fat.'

'What's he look like?'

'Hard to say, Patron. He seems to have no face.'

'No face?'

'Whoever did for him seems to have made a thorough job of it. Shot several times in the face and several times in the back of his head. It just about demolished his features.'

Pel grimaced. He didn't like messy murders. 'What about his papers?' he asked. 'Don't *they* give any indication?'

'No, Patron,' Darcy said. 'They're missing.'

'Clothes?'

'Not a chance, Patron.'

'Why not?'

'He isn't wearing any. At least nothing apart from undershirt, pants and socks.'

Pel stared. 'You don't usually undress before getting yourself murdered,' he said. 'At least, men don't. Especially in this weather. You could catch your death – '

He stopped, realising what he'd said. Darcy grinned.

'Somebody did, Patron.'

They climbed slowly. Darcy was driving carefully because of the snow on the road, and it took them until daylight to get anywhere near Butte-Avelan.

'Where did it happen?' Pel asked.

'Private estate called Bussy-la-Fontaine. Between Orgny and Savoie St Juste. In the Forest of Orgny.'

'Who's it belong to?'

'Guy called Piot. Paul-Edouard Piot.'

'Do we know him?'

'Shouldn't think so. He's fairly new here. He has a food-store in Chatillon and a factory in Dôle. He also has a few business interests in Paris and a second-hand book store in Dijon.'

'What's he doing at Butte-Avelan?'

'I gather he grew tired of fighting the unions and went in for this instead. He bought the place three years ago from a Madame Heurion, the widow of the previous owner. She preferred to live in a town and wanted to join her daughter in St Malo.'

'Where did you get all this?'

'Massu, the brigadier in charge of the sub-station at Orgny.'

'Isn't he the big chap? Bad-tempered?'

'Quick-tempered would be nearer.'

'How does he know all this?'

'He gets up to Bussy-la-Fontaine now and again. I get the impression Piot's not ungenerous with refreshment and it's a lovely spot in summer.'

'What is it? A farm?'

'No. Forestry. The wood goes for pulp, pit props and telegraph poles. Piot employs a garde forestier to look after it but he's about due for retirement and, according to Massu, Piot's decided that when he finally leaves he's going to run the place on his own.'

'Who found the body?'

'The garde.'

Pel stared gloomily at the grey-white landscape. 'Anybody else up there apart from the garde?'

'Just his wife and the owner, Piot.'

'What about *his* wife?'

'He hasn't got one. He's a bachelor.'

The road was climbing through the forest now. The leaves were brown and withered-looking, and the grass stuck in long spikes through the grey coating of melting snow. Occasionally they saw the eyes of some animal, and it came as a surprise to Pel because he'd always imagined that every scrap of wildlife in France had long since been killed by huntsmen. He'd seen them himself only the month before going out armed to the teeth with everything but anti-tank guns to stand in groups at the corners of every field and every crossroads, waiting to blast off at anything that moved. He'd thought at the time that it was a wonder a lot of them didn't shoot each other. Some of them did, of course.

The road curved round the top of the hill on to the bare high plains of the Côte d'Or, and they turned towards Savoie St Juste. A police car was waiting by the roadside and, as Darcy's lights caught it, a man in uniform jumped out to direct them down a long winding drive like a tunnel through the trees.

As the car came to a halt by the house a policeman, stamping his feet in the cold by the small cream Renault van from the Orgny sub-station, pointed to Massu, waiting in the doorway, looking like an ox in his thick clothing. He was a bull-like man with a dark meridional face and a chest like a wardrobe. Pel knew him well. He was a good policeman with a well-conducted district, though Pel suspected that he didn't always wait for the courts and preferred at times to deal out his own punishments.

'This way, sir,' he said, his black eyes and dark skin curiously menacing in the poor light.

They set off walking through the trees. The path was wide enough for a car; and its surface, where the snow had been tramped away by the police, was covered with twigs, old pine cones and the mulch of fallen leaves. It was bitterly cold, with a damp and chilling wind coming through the trees to set the branches above them crackling and creaking and shedding snow. Pel was already convinced he'd started a cold.

A few hundred yards from the house, in a small opening off the road, there was a small calvary. It was just a simple stone cross on a plinth to which a metal plate bearing several names had been screwed.

Behind it, a canvas screen had been erected. Inside it, Minet, the police surgeon, was bending over the body. He looked up at Pel as he appeared.

'You won't need a report from me for this,' he said.

'I'll have one, nevertheless,' Pel said. 'What happened?'

'There appear to be six shots in the head. Three in the face. Three more from behind. Those from behind smashed in the skull and blew out the face. Those fired from in front completed the ruin.'

Pel stared at the body. It was that of a well-built man, the flesh already slate-grey with death, and it wore short underpants, a sleeveless undershirt and black socks. It was covered by a thin layer of wet snow.

'Any marks on the clothing?'

'None that I can see. There might be, of course, under the blood.'

Pel studied the smashed pulp of the head. An eye, glazed now, stared out at him from the ruin, and short, thinning, grey-blond hair stood stiffly upright with the dried blood.

'Any other wounds?'

'His throat's been cut.'

Pel's jaw dropped. 'For the love of God! With six bullets in his head?'

'They probably did the throat first. We'll know when we get him back.'

Pel frowned. 'An execution, do you think?'

'Have we any gangsters round here?'

From what he read in the papers, Pel had a feeling that the world was swarming with gangsters, kidnappers, terrorists and murderers, all of whom practiced their trade for no other purpose than to prevent ageing detective inspectors like himself on the verge of retirement from getting any rest.

'There are *always* gangsters,' he said flatly. 'If somebody opens a bookmaker's office and his runners operate on another bookmaker's area, they end up brawling. That's gangsterism. If three kids get together to pinch another kid's ball, *that's* gangsterism, too. The world's full of it and it isn't getting less.'

He rubbed his nose and fought to resist the impulse to light a cigarette. 'Doesn't seem to be much blood on the ground,' he commented.

The doctor looked up. 'He wasn't killed here,' he said. 'That's one thing that's certain.'

'Why dump him here then?'

'Far as possible from the village.'

Pel stared about him. Beyond the path and the small opening where he stood, the forest was thick, and the undergrowth a mat of bushes, twigs and fallen branches.

'If I wanted to dump someone,' he said slowly, 'I wouldn't choose a spot only a couple of hundred metres from a dwelling house.' He gestured at the trees. 'I'd have dumped him in there.'

two

The photographers had arrived now, with Leguyader, from the Lab, who looked as peeved as Pel about being dragged out at that time of day. He and his men, with the aid of the police, would go over the area looking for anything that might give a clue to the dead man's identity, why he'd been dumped there, and who had killed him.

The wind had increased and flurries of sleet kept coming to make the snow more slushy. Moving branches showered the waiting men with small wet douches of snow, and they all looked frozen, their noses red against their white faces, their features drawn and strained.

None more than Pel. He'd put on so many clothes he could hardly move his arms, but the cold still crept insidiously through, and standing there, waiting for results, in a wind that was blasting its way across the snowy uplands all the way from the Baltic, was sheer agony.

He watched Leguyader, leaning over the body with him, his teeth clenched against the cold.

'What sort of gun?' he asked.

'Impossible to tell until we find the bullets,' Leguyader said. 'Some would go straight through the head after the first shots, but there should be one in there somewhere.'

'Any idea of size?'

'Three-eight. Something like that.'

'There are thousands of those about,' Darcy said.

'Including all those carried by the police,' Leguyader pointed out.

'Or stolen from the police,' Pel said. 'There are two of them at this moment around St Etienne. Anybody could have done it.'

'Including a policeman,' Massu said.

'Why would a policeman shoot him?' Darcy asked.

'Perhaps he'd annoyed the policeman,' Massu said.

While he waited for Leguyader to finish, Pel bent to read the plaque on the plinth of the cross. 'Fussillés par les Nazis,' it said. '7 Septembre, 1944.' The date was followed by nine names.

'What happened to them?' he asked.

Massu grunted. 'They're buried in the churchyard at Orgny. They still talk about it sometimes.'

Pel stared again at the plaque. 'One's a woman.'

'Yes.'

'Légion d'Honneur, too. Know anything about her?'

Massu's dark face changed. 'Only what I've heard in Orgny,' he said. 'The older men still talk about her.'

'What was so special about her?'

'She was brave.' Massu paused. 'At least, so I heard. Her man was killed at Sedan or somewhere in 1940, so she joined the Resistance. She became one of the toughest fighters in the area. She killed dozens of the bastards, they say.'

'Germans?'

'Who else?'

Pel studied the sergeant. 'You like this place, don't you?'

Massu's shoulders moved. 'It's my district. I look after it.'

'Did your parents come from these parts?'

'No. From the south. I've still got relatives down there, I believe.' Massu gestured. 'But I know how people feel.'

Pel stared about him. 'Come up here often?'

Massu shrugged again. 'Just to see Piot or Grévy, the garde. That's all. There was a bit of fuss with their neighbour,

Laco Matajcek, at Vaucheretard. That's the next farm to the west. He's a Czech. He came before the war and married a French girl. The farm was derelict and people tried to help him, but he's a bit of a shyster and it's still derelict. He's got no friends. He tried to pinch land from this estate in the days of Monsieur Heurion and I had to come up to ask a few questions and serve notices. The action's still going on.'

'Know anything about this garde who found the body?'

'Grévy?' Massu's heavy shoulders moved. 'He's been around a long time.'

'How about the owner of the place, Piot?'

'Bit of a mystery man.' Massu shrugged. 'Keeps to himself. Moved out here permanently last year. Up to then he spent most of his time in Dôle where his works are.'

'Why isn't he married?'

Masau grinned. 'Perhaps he can get it without.'

'Does he have girlfriends?'

'If he does, I've never heard of them.'

'Boyfriends?'

'Never heard of any. He seems normal enough. Shoots. Drives fast cars. Went around with his secretary a lot.'

'This secretary: what's her name?'

'Jacquemin. Marie-Claire Jacquemin.'

'Married?'

'No.' Massu's grin came again. 'So it's not her husband we found, and Piot didn't do it to get rid of him.'

Pel frowned. 'What's her address?'

'Somewhere in Dôle. You could get it from the factory. He still owns it, but he leaves it now to a manager. She still works there. She's quite important. He made her a director, I'm told. Partly to make sure the place's run honestly.' Massu's wide mouth lifted again. 'Partly, perhaps, for services rendered.'

'You'd better find out about her, Darcy.'

'Right, Patron.'

'And now let's go and see the garde.'

13

Bussy-la-Fontaine had been converted from a farmhouse and was built in local stone, with wine-coloured beams and ochre plaster. Heavy tiles covered the roof which was overhung by huge oaks almost bare of leaves. On either side were the remains of old walls, tufted with withered grass. At the end of one of them was a group of outbuildings and barns which had been converted into garages, and, separate, just beyond the end of the other was the cottage of the garde, with a wired-off area for chickens and a small fenced patch where an Alsatian guard dog stared angrily at them. The area between the walls had been sanded and converted into a courtyard, and what had once been a horse trough contained earth and the withered remains of the summer's geraniums.

The garde's cottage was over-decorated with calendars and pictures and coloured mirrors, and there was a big television in the corner. As Pel appeared the garde stood up. He was in his middle fifties and dwarfed even Massu. But this was chiefly because he was tall where Massu was not, and he had a belly like a wash tub and enormous thick-fingered hands. A woman stood behind him, a little younger but still good-looking, fully-dressed like the big man and wearing an overcoat.

'Albert Grévy,' the big man said. 'I'm the garde. This is my wife, Françoise.'

He reached for a bottle and placed it on the table. 'Marc,' he said.

Pel eyed it dubiously. So far, with one he'd had in the car with Darcy on the way up this made three since he'd got up and he hadn't eaten a thing yet. By evening he'd be in agonies with indigestion. He wished he were a superintendent, or even the Commissaire, or better still, retired.

'Santé,' he said, and sank the marc.

As Grévy swallowed his own drink, his wife, standing near the gas cooker, shifted on her feet.

'You've been told by the doctor to get weight off,' she said. 'That'll not do it.'

Grévy gestured. It was an indifferent gesture, a dismissive gesture, as if he'd never taken any notice of her and never would.

Pel looked at him. 'I believe you found the body,' he said.

The garde nodded. 'Yes,' he said. 'About four o'clock.'

'Know him?'

'No.'

Pel paused and forced himself to resist the temptation of lighting a cigarette. Instead he took out the little roller device and pushed tobacco into it to produce a bent-looking cigarette of infinite thinness and not too sturdy a character. As he lit it, it gave off the usual shower of sparks and a puff of smoke, and vanished in one drag.

Grévy pushed a packet of Gauloises across the table. 'Better have one of these,' he said.

Pel stared at him resentfully. 'I'm trying to cut it out,' he said. But he took one, nevertheless, and inhaled it thankfully.

He moved to the fireplace and stood with his back to the blaze, warming his behind, aware that he was keeping the heat from everybody else but cold enough not to care.

'Was he found at the calvary?' he asked.

'Yes.' Grévy poured more drinks.

'And the body? Propped up? Lying down?'

'Just lying there. On its back.'

'Notice any footprints?' Darcy asked.

'No. Just fresh snow.'

'Do you allow people to visit the calvary?' Pel asked.

'Yes,' Grévy said. 'You can drive there from the village.' He moved his big hands in a gesture. 'Nobody ever goes there these days.'

Pel looked up at him. With his black eyes and narrow face, and his flat forehead with its plastered-down hair, he looked like a cobra.

15

'Then what were *you* doing there?' he asked. 'At four o'clock in the morning.'

For a moment the garde's big face was blank, then he began to bluster.

'There's been some chicken stealing going on round here lately,' he said. 'The dog started barking and I went out to make sure they were all right.'

'Where do you keep the chickens?'

'Back of the house.'

'So why go down to the calvary?'

The garde gestured. 'I thought I saw a light among the trees.'

'What was it?'

The garde gestured again. 'I'm not sure now that there was one,' he said. 'I just saw a flash of light. But there was still a bit of moon and it could have been shining on the snow or on a puddle between the trees. I was thinking of the chickens.'

'And you went to investigate and found the body?'

'Yes.'

'No sign of tracks?'

'No. The snow had fallen.'

'Whoever put him there,' Massu observed, 'must have been a strong man.' His glance flickered to the bulk of the garde.

'Could he have been driven there?'

'There were no tyre marks.'

'There wouldn't be,' Darcy said. 'It's been freezing for days. The ground under the snow would be too hard to show anything.'

Pel stood silently, toying with his pencil. 'Go near the calvary the previous day at all?' he asked.

Grévy frowned. 'No,' he said. 'I was working on the tractor most of the morning in the garage. In the afternoon I went down to Orgny to get spare parts.'

Pel frowned. 'Any strangers about here lately?' he asked.

'No.'

'Nobody who might have been this chap we found?'

'We don't often get people up here,' Grévy said. 'Though they're allowed to visit the shrine, they're not allowed to wander in the woods. There are a lot of young trees about and they could damage them. When they're fully grown we sell them to timber merchants. They bring in their own workmen to cut them down. They're usually Czechs.'

'Czechs?' Pel looked up. 'This guy, Matajcek, next door's a Czech, isn't he?'

'Yes. He worked on the woodcutting at one time. That's how he spotted the land next door.'

'Look into him, Darcy,' Pel said. 'Who do you use for this wood-cutting?'

'Sordet Brothers from Chatillon.'

'Any other firms who use Czechs?'

'Only Jacques Peyroutin, from Langres.'

'Look them up, Darcy.' Pel looked again at the garde. 'How about you? How did you come to work up here?'

Grévy shrugged his big shoulders. 'I worked in a factory in Chaumont but I was never well. They told me I needed fresh air. Here I'm always out of doors. I'm my own boss. Or more or less. Monsieur Piot's easy to work for.'

'He's not been at it long, has he? Does he understand it?'

Grévy smiled for the first time, but it was curiously mirthless. 'He does his farming with a digger,' he said.

'What do you mean?'

'Well, he's not like Monsieur Heurion. Monsieur Heurion knew the game inside-out.' Grévy's sombre face melted into another smile. 'This one seems to prefer reshaping the place to replanting it. He's dug a dam, changed the roads in three places, and removed about four banks. I think he just likes to drive the digger.'

'Did he ever have any strange visitors?'

The garde looked puzzled and Pel tried to explain. 'Did anyone ever visit him who didn't seem to fit?'

Grévy still didn't grasp what he was getting at and Pel lost his temper. 'If you saw one of the Baader-Meinhoff Gang or the Red Brigade visiting the Archbishop of Paris,' he snapped, 'that would be strange, wouldn't it? Ever see anybody like that here?'

'Baader-Meinhoff?'

Pel glared.

Grévy shrugged. 'Well, the Archbishop of Paris never visited here.'

Pel decided to let it go. Either Grévy was more stupid than he looked or he was being clever.

'Contact the Chief, the Palais de Justice and the Proc,' he said quietly to Darcy. 'Let them know what's happening. Go down to Orgny and use Massu's telephone. I'll go and see Piot.'

The courtyard was wet and the sand that stuck to Pel's shoes was tramped into the kitchen of the main residence. Piot was waiting for him, a small rugged-looking man with a fresh outdoor complexion, broad shoulders, a good-natured expression and a clear air of being in charge of himself. He was wearing city clothes.

He was fishing in a cupboard and as Pel appeared he straightened up with a bottle in his fist.

'I was just about to leave for Paris,' he said. 'I'm Piot. It's cold out there, Inspector, so perhaps you'd welcome a glass of something warm. The spirit we distil here could be used in a blow torch.'

He sloshed plum brandy into glasses and they drank. Pel felt it moving down into his stomach and spreading out fanwise into all the little roots and branches of his system. It was going to be a terrible day, he knew, with missed meals, and too much to drink in an effort to keep warm.

Piot had stirred up a fire of logs on a high, raised hearth and it was blazing enough to make the place warm, though there were still murderous draughts howling round the place.

Pel sat down at the table. 'I've just been talking to the garde,' he said.

Piot's face twisted in a small smile. 'About me, I expect,' he said. 'And now it's my turn to talk about him.'

Pel shrugged. 'It's the only way we can find out about people.'

'What do you want to know?'

'Well, for a start, what do you do here?'

'I try to improve the place. It was a mess when I took it over.'

'A mess? Grévy says that the previous owner, Heurion, was pretty good.'

'Well, I suppose he was.' Piot smiled. 'But he was old-fashioned. He was seventy-six when he died.'

'What do you do?'

'Drainage. I concentrate on drainage. It's a big thing these days. A lot of land's been reclaimed by drainage.'

'Here?'

'Not yet. But it will be. Some of the bottom lands are wet. Then there are roads. They have to be maintained so machinery can move about. And dams. I've built one already. I've got a digger. A Poclain.'

'Go near the calvary yesterday at all?'

Piot smiled. 'Not likely. It was too cold. I helped Grévy with the tractor in the morning. In the afternoon, I was here at the kitchen table working. Reports. That sort of thing. Anything else?'

'Yes. Your girlfriend. The one who was your secretary.'

Piot laughed. 'That's all over. She's happy. I'm happy. We agreed to part. I made her a good present and she's never bothered me since.'

'What do you know of Grévy?'

'He came with the place. He'd had chest trouble. Asthma. Something like that. I can't remember exactly. He'd been working at Chaumont and been advised to get an outdoor job.'

'Is he honest?'

Piot smiled. 'Perhaps he sells logs to his friends. Perhaps he drinks my wine. Perhaps he eats the eggs from the chickens whose feed I pay for. In fact, I'm sure he does. But those are normal perks, aren't they, in the same way that the clerks in my works at Dôle take home my office paper to write their private letters on, then send them off stamped by the office franking machine. Everybody has perks of some sort.'

'Is that all?'

'All I can guess at.'

'He says he was out there at four o'clock when he found the body. That's pretty early.'

'Not for Grévy.'

'Does he usually go out at that time?'

'Invariably. Then, just to prove he's out and about, he starts the tractor and leaves it running by the gate so it'll wake me up and I'll know he's on the ball.'

'Is he good at his job?'

'He does all I ask.'

'Sober?'

Piot smiled again. 'Not always. He likes to drive down to Orgny at lunch time and in the evenings. His wife goes on at him about it. I hear them from here sometimes. He wrote off a new car he bought coming home in the summer. He walked the rest of the way and by the time Sergeant Massu arrived he was stone cold sober and full of black coffee. They breath-tested him, of course, but by that time what he hadn't got rid of had dispersed.'

'At least he shows initiative.'

'Oh, don't let him fool you.' Piot's smile grew wider. 'Now he's big and fat. But when he was young he was just big. He was taken prisoner in 1940 and he escaped. He killed a guard dog and a guard, and on the way back a German policeman. He arrived home fit and well and promptly joined the Resistance!'

'How do you know this?'

'I was in the Resistance, too.'

'You don't look old enough.'

'I wasn't. I was sixteen and a half when the war ended. But I had my moments, too. I fell for a girl I met cycling. She was pretty, she was French, and she was friendly. I discovered later she was in the pay of the Germans. I was lucky. I was warned about her in time.'

'Your family have always lived in these parts?'

Piot's smile was warm. 'I'm a Burgundian. Anybody with a name ending in "ot's" a good Burgundian.'

Pel sniffed. He was a good Burgundian too, and proud of it. He was so Burgundian, in fact, that when foreigners, talking of wines, mentioned Bordeaux, he was inclined to ask 'What's that?'

He rose and moved round the table to the side farthest from the fire. With all the sweaters he'd put on, he was beginning to feel a bit like a boiled turkey.

'Ever see Grévy with anybody around here?' he asked.

Piot got the point at once. 'No,' he said. 'The police called occasionally on enquiries, because this place is lonely, and they sometimes arrive to ask if we've seen someone in the woods they're looking for.'

Pel's mind went at once to the four men who'd murdered the police at St Symphorien. 'Do you?'

'No. Though sometimes I bump into Emile Heutelet. He owns L'Hermitage, the farm adjoining my land. He's retired now and his sons run the place. But he doesn't enjoy doing nothing so he does deliveries for the wine warehouse at Savoie St Juste. He calls at outlying farms en route to see old friends and take an occasional glass of wine.' Piot paused. 'And, so it's said, because he's a handsome man still, to indulge a little with a wife when her husband's away.'

'Anybody else ever come here?'

'Perhaps another garde forestier or someone from one of the other estates. Farm machinery agents trying to sell something. Pumps, tractors. That sort of thing. We get them as well. But not many. It's one of Madame Grévy's complaints that she never sees anyone.

'Does *she* have boyfriends?' Pel asked. 'When her husband goes to the bar?'

Piot shrugged, his eyes suddenly blank and shuttered. 'You'd better ask her,' he said. 'It's none of my business.'

'It's mine,' Pel pointed out.

'I still think you'd better ask *her.*'

three

Orgny stood at the bottom of the winding hill that came down from Butte-Avelan and, like so many places in that part of Burgundy, it had a lost look, full of old crooked buildings built of heavy timbers and enormous grey stones. Yet its few shops were up-to-date and there was a garage and a hotel with a large bar where, if the landlord was in a good mood and it wasn't too much trouble, you could put up for the night. It had been exactly the same for generations, cut off from the mainstream of events, so that the names on the new gravestones in the churchyard were the same names that were in the old registers, families which had been born there for centuries, receiving their Confirmation and their first Communion there before marrying and finally dying and being buried there. Only nowadays, with motor cars and television, was it beginning to change and its people getting the itch to leave.

There was a lot of snow at the bottom of the hill, as if it had drifted on the wind, and Darcy almost slid into the village. The street was empty except for the owner of the bar, red-nosed and muffled to the eyes, who was sweeping the pavement outside his door.

Driving into the Maine, Darcy swung his car round the side past the police office and parked at the back alongside a small Renault which he recognised as belonging to Massu's constable, Weyl.

'They're both out,' a voice called as he climbed from the car and, looking up, he saw a man in the garden adjoining the police parking area.

'I know,' Darcy said.

'There's been a murder.'

Darcy looked at the speaker, who was standing by a chicken run, holding a bucket of seed. At his feet a few scrawny birds pecked.

'How do you know?' Darcy said.

'They told me as they went. If you want to use a telephone, you can use ours. I'm the postmaster. Georges Vallois-Dot.'

Darcy studied him for a second. He was a tall man, gangling, moustached and spectacled, who stooped from years of bending over a desk. His face was pale with the pallor of a man who spent his days indoors, and he had an uncertain air as though he had never in his life been sure of himself.

'They always use our phone if theirs goes out of order,' he pointed out. 'It's official, you see. The post office. Government, just the same.'

As Darcy turned away, the postmaster spoke again. 'Who is it?' he asked.

Darcy gave him a cold look but it didn't seem to put him off and he went on chattering in his nervous manner as he tossed handfuls of seed at the chickens.

'We've never had anything like this before here,' he said. 'Accidents occasionally. Sometimes a lorry runs away coming down the hill. Those heavy ones, pulling trailers. They come down the bypass flat out, to get up speed to go up the other side and if someone just happens to come out from the village, wham, they jack-knife. It's a wonder nobody's killed. You're very welcome to use our telephone. I shan't listen.'

'You won't get a chance, mon vieux,' Darcy smiled. 'I shan't be using it. I have the key to the sub-station.'

The Chief wanted to know all the details and the Proc asked if they'd arrested anyone, while the Palais de Justice, who seemed not to possess a map, wanted to know exactly where it was and how to get there. By the time Darcy had finished and returned to Bussy-la-Fontaine, Pel was ready to leave. There were policemen everywhere by now and the press had arrived – the usual lot, Sarrazin, the freelance; Henriot, from *Le Bien Public;* and Fiabon, from *France Dimanche* and *Paris Soir,* looking for something juicy.

'Is it anything to do with the murder of those two cops at St Symphorien, Inspector?' Sarrazin asked.

'I shouldn't think so,' Pel said. 'See Massu. He can tell you all we know.'

Darcy appeared from the car. 'Where to, Patron?' he asked.

Pel gestured. 'Let's go and see this farmer – Heutelet. He may have heard or seen something.'

Nosjean was in the back of the car, waiting for a lift back to the city, and he was dragging on a cigarette as if his life depended on it.

'What's wrong with you?' Pel asked. 'Got the cafard? Or is it just your girlfriend?'

Nosjean shifted uncomfortably. 'Girlfriend, Patron.'

'Chucked you again?'

'Yes.'

Pel eased himself into his seat. 'I thought this time it was deathless,' he said.

'It was.' Nosjean sighed. 'But last night she said it was finished.' The fields of L'Hermitage, the farm next door, touched against Piot's forest land. It was a big farm, well run, with cared-for approach roads and borders, and well-repaired buildings. Emile Heutelet was still a handsome man with a strong body, white hair and a ready smile, and since retirement, with the farmhouse now occupied by his two sons and their families, he lived in a wing at the back with his wife.

'I heard no shots,' he said. 'But you could hardly expect me to, could you? We're in a valley here and Bussy-la-Fontaine's high up. Sound plays funny tricks. When you're three storeys up you don't hear the noise of the traffic. It's the same when you're three storeys below. Sound doesn't go round corners.'

'See any strangers about?'

'No.' Heutelet gestured. 'You can't get out here without a car, so it's always been quiet. That's why I was chosen to run the Resistance during the war.'

'Did you?'

'For two years. We've not had as many people here since 1944, when the Germans looted Baron de Mougy's château at Sainte Monique. They hid the stuff in the woods up here somewhere.'

Pel had heard the story. 'Was it ever found?'

'No. The woods were full of German police and they did a lot of digging but nothing turned up.'

It seemed sense, while they were there, to call on Laco Matajcek who owned the land called Vaucheretard on the other side of Bussy-la-Fontaine. If he was close enough to try to steal its land, he was probably close enough to see someone about.

Vaucheretard was about a hundred feet higher on the next hill, and just that much colder. The snow had changed to rain and it was sluicing down when they arrived. The place looked like a derelict heap of bricks and timbers dumped by out-of-work builders; Pel took one look at it and promptly lit a Gauloise. This was no time for worrying about cancer, he decided, and the roller machine was best left in his pocket.

Matajcek opened the kitchen door at their knock but he obviously had no intention of asking them in. Standing in the rain, Pel put his questions, but for replies received only monosyllables. Matajcek had seen nobody, never did see anybody, and never wanted to see anybody.

Beyond him, through the curtain of rain drops from the lintel, they could see into the kitchen. It contained a long, old-fashioned sofa covered with filthy blankets, and even at the door they caught the stink of dirt, decaying food and chickens.

'How about Madame Matajcek?' Pel asked. 'Would she perhaps have seen anyone?'

Matajcek, a square-shouldered man with pale piercing eyes, had the flat face of a Russian moujik, and his expression showed a clear resentment at their presence and a hostility towards Pel he did nothing to hide.

His wife wasn't there, he told them in a thick Slav accent, and when they persisted, he admitted only that she had gone, so that it finally dawned on them that she'd probably gone off with another man, and that perhaps it was from this fact that Matajcek's resentment sprang. No man welcomed questions when his wife had just run out on him.

As they left, Pel's nose wrinkled, and Massu smiled. 'He's not known for washing a lot,' he said.

'What does he live on?' Pel asked.

Massu's big shoulders shrugged. 'A few cattle, a few pigs, a few chickens. He grows his own foodstuff and spends all his time here. Just goes occasionally to Chatillon for tools, or to Orgny or Savoie St Juste for paraffin or coffee – that sort of thing.'

'Know him well?'

Massu scowled. 'I tangled with him once or twice. Over Heurion's boundary, for instance. He once threatened me with a shotgun.'

'What happened?'

'He ended up flat on his back.'

Back at the Hôtel de Police, Pel stalked to his room. Almost at once, the telephone rang. It was Brisard, the juge d'instruction, wanting to know what was happening.

Brisard was an interfering busybody who couldn't leave things alone. Inflexible, guided by principles, and determined to be determined, he always failed to be because he was a weak character.

'Nothing yet,' Pel said. 'We've only just heard about it.'

'I'd better go up there and have a look round.'

'Yes,' Pel said. 'You had.'

Perhaps Brisard would get wet feet, he thought, and, with a bit of luck, pneumonia and die. He didn't like Brisard. He was a tall overweight man, young for his office, who laid heavy stress on his devotion to his family. Pel knew it was all eyewash because he'd once seen him in Beaune with a woman who'd turned out to be the widow of a police officer.

'Is there nothing to identify the victim?' Brisard asked.

'So far, nothing, judge. Underclothing and socks. That's all.'

'Who put you on to it?'

'The garde. He was found on private land.'

'Is it worth having the garde brought in?'

'Not yet, judge. It's too early.'

'If only that place could talk!'

If only *people* could manage to talk, Pel thought bitterly.

As he put the telephone down, it rang again immediately. This time it was Doctor Minet.

Pel could just imagine him at his marble slab, busy at the autopsy. He was cheerful and brisk and liked to chain-smoke as he worked. Sometimes Pel had to be present when he carved up the cadavres that came in, and he always stood well back, nauseated and trying not to look.

'Our friend in the Forêt d'Orgny,' Minet said. 'Dead about eight hours, I think.'

'Go on.'

'Fair complexion. From the north probably. Certainly not a Meridional.'

'Anything else?'

'Six wounds in the head. You saw them. I don't have to describe them. None of them killed him. It was cutting his throat that did that.'

Pel was silent for a moment. 'Anything else?' he asked.

'Tattoo mark on right forearm.' Minet sounded pleased with himself. 'Old wound in left calf. Looked like a bullet wound.'

'How old?'

'Oh, mon dieu! Thirty years. Forty perhaps. From the war, I imagine.'

'There must have been a hundred thousand Frenchmen wounded in the war,' Pel said flatly. 'Of which I imagine perhaps ten thousand were hit in the leg. That doesn't help us much. Is that the lot?'

'Well preserved,' Minet went on. 'Probably good-looking in his youth. The nose isn't disfigured and it's neat. Good jaw-line. That's about all I can tell you. Fair hair, slightly reddish, but now going grey. Blue eyes. About one metre eighty tall. Well-built. Running to fat, but just according to his age.'

'Teeth?'

'His own.'

'I'll send Nosjean over for the details. Perhaps some dentist will know who he is. And have that tattoo photographed and sent to the Lab, will you? What about the bullet?'

'We found two altogether. One in the ground. One in the remains of the skull. I've sent them to Ballistics. I think they were from a Mathurin-Walther .38.'

'Like mine?'

Minet chuckled. 'You didn't do it, did you?'

The weather continued to improve during the evening, but even at that you could hardly have called it good. The temperature rose a little and the sleety rain effectively cleared the grey slush from the streets. By late afternoon the city was no longer beautiful under its mantle of white and was just cold and cheerless, the lights from the shops reflected on the black and shining pavements.

Darcy's check on the forestry workers proved a dead loss. The Langres firm had stopped using them three years before and Sordet Brothers at Chatillon only employed four, all of whom had a cast-iron alibi. Even the photographs of the dead man's tattoo that Nosjean brought back from the Lab showed very little. It consisted of a curve with, above it, the remains of two straight lines ending in what looked like double circles. Beneath it was what appeared to be the remains of a number from which they could just make out an 0. Or was it part of a 6, or a 9 or even an 8? Or could the marks even have been letters?

'Anchor?' Darcy suggested, staring at it over Pel's shoulder. 'With the name of a ship? Could he have been a sailor?'

'In Burgundy?' Pel asked. 'You're about as far from the sea here as you can get in Europe.'

'He might have been a sailor during the war, Patron. He's about the right age.'

'He might also be one of that lot from St Etienne who shot those cops. They've nothing to lose now, and Doc Minet thinks it was done with a .38. Two .38s are missing.'

'We're two hundred kilometres from St Etienne, Patron.'

'Two hours' driving time,' Pel scowled. 'No trouble at all.'

'But why undress him and blow his head to bits? Why cut his throat?'

It didn't stand up and even Pel had to accept it.

'Besides,' Darcy said. 'Men of his age don't go in for robbing banks. They don't move fast enough. You have to be nippy on your feet for that.'

As Pel sat back and took out his little cigarette-making machine, Darcy pushed a packet of Gauloises across. 'Why not have a real one?' he asked.

Pel made a great show of ignoring him. 'Get on to Missing Persons,' he said. 'Find out if anybody fitting the description we have has vanished from home.'

'It isn't usually men of fifty-odd who disappear from home,' Darcy said dryly. 'It's usually kids. Young girls.'

'You'll know something about that, of course.'

Darcy was unmoved. 'I'm a great one for breaking up homes,' he said.

He was only boasting, of course, because he always seemed to know exactly when to back off, something that stirred the envious Nosjean to cataclysms of bitterness.

Pel was bent over his little gadget of rollers and rubber. The operation took a great deal of time and Darcy watched, fascinated.

'Is it because you're afraid of cancer or for the exercise?' he asked.

Pel gave him a sour look. 'I've nearly given them up,' he said. 'I've cut them down a lot.'

'What to?'

Pel sighed. 'About twenty million a day.'

Pel drove home slowly in the dark. He'd tried ringing Leguyader to find out if the Lab had discovered anything, but Leguyader, while prepared to work flat out if necessary, wasn't prepared to accommodate anybody that much, and Pel felt frustrated.

It was not an uncommon emotion with Pel. Though he was one of the most successful detectives outside Paris or Marseilles, he suffered from a permanent feeling of failure.

His car was old, his house was falling down, nobody loved him because he'd never married and had no family, he was approaching his pension and was still only an inspector living in abject poverty and great discomfort. The fact that he'd stacked away his wages over the years with the parsimony of a peasant, investing them carefully for his still far-distant old age, completely failed to be taken into account. According to Pel, Inspector Evariste Clovis Désiré Pel was a sad case.

Even his name was a load. Every time he had to produce his papers to have his badge renewed, every time he had to pay his taxes or change his driving licence – there it was staring out at him. He often thought it was the reason he'd never married.

He parked the car in the street outside his house. The slamming of the driver's door sounded like someone hurling a tin can into the gutter. Only a poverty-striken overworked inspector would have a battered Peugeot as he did. The men he sent to prison always seemed to drive Mercs.

The house was shuddering to the sound of the television. Madame Routy was a television addict. For Madame Routy there were only two positions in the volume control. Off and full blast. It sounded like the charge of Ney's cuirassiers at Mont St Jean.

As usual she occupied le confort anglais, the best chair in the house, and she looked up indifferently.

'Your meal's in the oven,' she said.

Pel went to the kitchen and opened the oven. As he took out the casserole dish he guessed the vegetables were frozen. Scooping the lot into the rubbish bucket under the sink, he decided to eat out. He fished out a cigarette packet from his pocket, hesitated, put it back and produced the little roller gadget. One day, he decided, he'd spend all weekend making cigarettes. He could end up on a Monday with enough for a whole month and the practice would make him an expert.

He fiddled about for ten minutes or so, put the result in his mouth, lit it and drew two unsatisfying puffs before taking it out and tossing it into the rubbish bucket after the casserole. Lighting a Gauloise, he decided it was probably better to die of cancer of the lung than overwrought nerves. The way he smoked, he thought, it was a wonder even the walls weren't cancerous. Perhaps, however, it was just a lot of doctors being neurotic, because he'd heard Albanians smoked from birth to old age, and cancer was unknown there.

Reassured, he set off for the city. The restaurant he chose was the Relais St Armand in the Avenue Maréchal Foch. It served good beer and a Muscadet that was sharp enough to take the enamel off your teeth, and he decided on an andouillette, the tripe sausage of the region.

As he waited, fiddling with the cigarette maker, the woman on the next table watched with interest. 'Why not try a real one?' she suggested, passing a silver-inlaid case across.

'Thank you, Madame,' Pel said with as much dignity as he could muster. 'I'm more than grateful. But I'm trying to give it up.'

When Pel's soup arrived, he ate it heartily. Despite the fact that he was a convinced dyspeptic, he still had a healthy appetite. When he'd finished the meal, he fished for his cigarettes, sighed, replaced them and took out the roller. The woman smiled and held up her case. He shook his head firmly.

'I must persevere, Madame,' he said.

The result was the same as usual and she laughed out loud. 'Do you ever catch fire?' she asked.

'Not too often,' Pel said grimly.

She passed the case across and he accepted sadly.

She was in her late thirties, he judged, with an unlined face, good features and deep violet eyes. He wished he could offer her Madame Routy's job.

'Perhaps you'll take a brandy with me,' he suggested.

She shook her head. 'I never touch it. I have to watch my weight.'

He expressed dutiful astonishment and said that he, too, had to try to keep fit.

'You are perhaps an athlete?' she asked.

Pel stared down at his incipient paunch. 'Madame, you have to be joking.'

'But no!' Her eyes widened. 'Why should I be? You look a fit, young man. It's a natural question.'

Pel was flattered. Fit! Young! It went to his head a little. 'I'm a policeman,' he confessed.

He waited for her to sneer. It was the usual thing. People sneered at you because you stood up to be shot at by terrorists or have your head broken by rioting students, or because you had a job that obviously wasn't paid enough and you had to be corrupt. Instead, she expressed polite interest.

'*I* have responsibilities to my job, too,' she said. 'I run a beauty salon.'

'Ah!' That probably explained her neat hair, her good make-up. 'You've probably heard of it: Nanette. In the Rue de la Liberté.' Pel had.

'I'm Nanette. Geneviève Faivre-Perret.'

'And your husband?'

'There isn't one. He's dead. That's why I'm Nanette. Otherwise I'd stay at home and get up late every morning.'

'Ah!' Pel was enjoying himself. 'Pel, Madame. Inspector Pel.' He wondered which of his three names to offer her – something which always bothered him – and decided on the first. 'Evariste Pel.'

They shook hands solemnly, then she began to collect her belongings and stood up. She had a figure like a dream. 'I have to go,' she said.

Pel watched her like a spaniel having its lunch taken away from it. At the door, she paused and smiled at him as she went out, and he settled back to stare at his coffee sunk in the blackest despondency.

Full of fantasies about getting rid of Madame Routy and offering the job to Madame Faivre-Perret, with the strict qualification that she never need get up early, he returned home. He was thoroughly disillusioned. It was nice to have fantasies, but perhaps a good job they never came off. Doubtless Madame Faivre-Perret had a temper and – if it were possible! – liked to have the television even louder than Madame Routy.

He went to bed deep in gloom. Downstairs Madame Routy was watching a programme on the kings of France that sounded like the storming of the Tuileries. It would go on to the last bitter minute, then there would be silence while she made a hot drink. Just as he was dropping off to sleep, she would charge – that was the only word for it – upstairs and smash up the bathroom as she prepared for bed. He knew she was only washing and cleaning her teeth and brushing her hair, but it always sounded as if she were wrecking the place and it was always a matter of great surprise to him the next day when he went in to find it still there, undamaged.

Sure enough, she did charge up the stairs just as he was dropping off and began, apparently, to hurl things at the bathroom walls. Madame Routy could make turning taps on and off sound like the liberation of Paris.

Eventually, the uproar died down and he heard her door slam. By this time he was wide awake, certain he'd never go to sleep again. He tried for a while to think of Madame Faivre-Perret and wondered if he might find an excuse to investigate the identity of the man at Bussy-la-Fontaine at her salon. He couldn't imagine how he possibly could.

He'd just dropped off again when the telephone went. The sound crashed round the room, rattling against the walls and bringing him upright in bed at once.

Snatching up the instrument he barked at it. 'Pel!'

It was Darcy, and Pel snarled at him. 'What is this?' he demanded. 'It's getting to be a habit.'

Darcy made soothing noises and Pel went on bitterly. 'I'd just got off to sleep,' he said. 'Don't I ever get any peace?' His martyrdom didn't seem to have got across, so he pushed it a little harder. 'You'll be telling me next that someone else's been attacked.'

'Yes, Patron – ' Pel felt sure that Darcy was smiling as he spoke ' – I will. Because somebody has. That chap Matajcek. He was discovered with a fractured skull outside his barn.'

four

'There seems to be a nut about,' Darcy said.

They stood in the rain outside a battered stone barn. The rain was coming down like stair rods now and they were all soaked to the skin.

They had passed the ambulance on the way up, jolting down the uneven lane and rolling through the puddles to send out waves of liquid mud from the wheels. If anything, the wind was colder than ever and it plastered their wet trousers to their legs, clammy and icy, as they tried to shelter from the weather.

Massu's constable, Weyl, making a last-minute prowl round in the hope that he might bump into whoever had dumped the body at the calvary, had called at Vaucheretard and found Matajcek lying outside his door in a puddle of water. The doctor he'd summoned from Savoie St Juste, was young, handsome, and cynical, and his report on Matajcek was simple and straightforward.

'What's wrong with him?' he said in answer to Pel's question. 'Easy. Fractured skull, old age and dirt. He's got a fractured skull because somebody hit him with something heavy and hard, he's suffering from old age because he was born a long time ago, and he was dirty because he never washed.'

Pel listened irritatedly. The only person entitled to be funny when Pel was around was Pel himself. 'What was he hit with?' he asked.

'Spade,' the doctor said. 'Plough share. Anvil. Side of a house. Take your pick. Hard, heavy and flat. That's as far as I can say at the moment. Because he was old, it's touch and go, and because he's dirty – and, mon dieu, how dirty! – he'll probably get gangrene and die of that.'

'*Is* he going to die?'

'Probably not. But it'll be a long time before he recovers enough to talk.'

Only two of the rooms of the derelict house were occupied, one the kitchen. There was no bathroom, and the cow byre alongside was as tumbledown as the house itself.

'It must be part of that bank robbery and the murder of those cops at St Symphorien,' Massu said in a flat voice. 'They must be working their way north past this district.'

Pel gave him a sour look. 'This trouble Matajcek had with Piot,' he asked. 'What happened?'

Massu shrugged. 'It was about boundaries,' he said. 'He'd pinched a bit of Piot's land. Carefully, you understand, and in Heurion's time. In a valley between where nobody goes much. But when he moved the fence, it put the stream on *his* side so his cattle could use it. He thought he could get away with it but Heurion wasn't that stupid. I had to deliver a notice to him to remove it.'

'Did he?'

'As far as I know, no. But Piot's taken it to court again since and judgement's been given for him, so that seems to be that.'

Leaving Nosjean to explore the place, Pel turned to the car. 'I'm going to Bussy-la-Fontaine,' he said. 'This time *they* might have seen someone. Keep your eyes open, Nosjean. Find out if there've been any strangers about.'

Nosjean blinked the rain from his eyelashes and spat it from his lips. He looked about him at the puddled farmyard and the ooze that had once been cow dung but had disintegrated under the rain into a yellow slime. A dejected-looking hen was picking about among the scattered chaff under a broken cart that was short of a wheel.

'Who do I ask, Patron?' He gestured at the tumbledown buildings, the mud, the broken gates, and the few cows making snuffling noises as they chewed their cud, mooing welcomes as they stared at them with their big soft eyes. 'Nobody ever comes here.'

'You never know your luck,' Pel said flatly. 'Somebody might. And we haven't got the weapon yet.'

There were still policemen by the calvary at Bussy-la-Fontaine with Misset.

'Patron,' Misset complained. 'I ought to be home. Not standing here getting my death of cold.'

'Why you particularly?' Pel asked tartly. 'I'm wet, too.'

'My wife needs me, Patron.'

'When's the baby due?'

'Three months time.'

Pel grunted. 'You ought to be home by then,' he said remorselessly. 'Have you found anything?'

Misset gave him a bitter look. 'No, Chief. There aren't any tracks. If someone brought the stiff up by car to dump him, it must have been done before the snow and while the ground was still hard from frost. There are no footprints – not identifiable, anyway – and just one tyre print down there.'

'What sort?'

Misset shrugged. 'Looks exactly the same as the ones on my own car,' he said. 'Michelin ZX 145-15.'

'Have you taken a cast?'

'Too wet at the moment, Chief. And that clot, Massu, put his foot on it. "Look at that, Massu," I said. "Where?" he said. "Right under your damned great hoof," I told him. There's enough to get a cast, though. I've covered it and taped it off. I'll get it as soon as the rain stops.' Misset brushed the rain from his face. 'It won't tell us much, though. That tyre's fitted on every small car in France – Renaults,

Citroën Dianes, the lot. They have 'em on the vans of every police sub-station in the country.'

Pel stared about him. There was still snow on the northern slopes but it had turned to grey slush now and inside the taped-off area there wasn't a single footprint. Pel frowned. He'd been a policeman long enough to know there was something odd about this case – that was, if you didn't call a man with his head almost blown to shreds and stripped to his underclothes odd already. It had a feel about it. As if somehow it weren't anchored in anything he understood.

'No signs of black magic?' he asked.

'Patron?' Misset looked startled.

Pel sighed. 'There've been some funny cases lately,' he said. 'People going in for the occult.'

Misset caught on. 'I've found nothing you could remotely connect with that sort of thing,' he said. 'They go in for feathers tied in a bunch, fires and so on, don't they? There's nothing here but pine cones and snow. And no fires.' He stamped his feet. 'I wish to God there *was* a fire.'

'You could always put a match to the barn,' Darcy suggested.

Pel frowned at the flippancy. 'Let's see if we can make a start by getting our man identified,' he said. 'Round the hotels. See if anybody's missing. Push it. Put Krauss on it. His chicken stealer's not been busy lately. Check as far south as Châlon-sur-Saône. As far north as Bussy-Rabutin. East to the Jura. West to Sémur. That ought to be enough. If the man was a commercial traveller – something of that sort – I doubt if he'd have come from further away than that. Not in one day. Not in this weather. He ought to come out of the woodwork somewhere.'

On the way back into the city, Pel sat silently. Darcy said nothing, waiting for him to speak. The rain lashing against the windscreen was swept away in miniature tidal waves by the wipers. Pel stirred at last, fiddled with his cigarette roller for a moment or two, put it away, dragged out a Gauloise, lit it and drew guiltily on it.

'See any connection?' he asked.

'Between Matajcek and our faceless friend?'

Pel nodded, his eyes dark and sad.

'Well, Matajcek was a Czech, and Czech timber workers have worked at Bussy-la-Fontaine.' Darcy's shoulders moved. 'Massu thinks it was those four who killed the cops at St Symphorien.'

Pel grunted. 'Massu's got solid stone between his ears,' he growled.

'Well, it's too big a coincidence to ignore,' Darcy said. 'And Matajcek's place is just the sort they look for. One occupant. No woman to gossip. Perhaps they turned up after we left yesterday.'

They stopped at Val-Suzon for a coffee and roll. Darcy suggested a brandy to warm them up and Pel didn't say no, because he liked brandy. On the other hand, he didn't say yes, either, because brandy didn't like him, so he merely grunted and let it roll over him.

Back at the office there was a message to call the Chief. Pel sighed and picked up the telephone. The Chief was worried.

'There's been a cry for help from St Etienne,' he said. 'Have we seen four bank robbers?'

He seemed to be urging Pel on to greater efforts and Pel frowned. 'I think we have enough troubles of our own,' he said, and recounted what had happened at Orgny.

There was a long silence. 'Could there be any connection with the St Symphorien shootings?' Encouraging noises came down the telephone. 'Keep your eyes open. If there's the slightest chance we'll have to call in St Etienne.'

As Pel put the telephone down, Doctor Minet rang. He sounded cheerful.

'I've finished with your stiff,' he said.

'Anything that might identify him?'

41

'Just the tattoo. And the old bullet wound in the right calf. You know about them.'

'Go on. There's more, I know.'

'Yes.' Minet laughed. 'He's no smoker by the look of him. There were no traces of nicotine in his lungs, and his fingers weren't yellowed. Yet there were traces on his teeth, which is odd. He'd been shot six times by a .38 calibre revolver. Three times in the face and three times in the back of the head, with the angle of the bullet moving upwards from the base of the spine.'

'Classic execution angle,' Pel observed.

'Except that his throat was cut first.'

Pel frowned and the doctor went on. 'From behind,' he said. 'They usually do it that way. Grab the hair and hold the head back with the left hand, to expose the throat, then sweep across the jugular with the knife in the right.'

'And the bullets?'

'He was dead when they were fired. Thrown forward, I expect. He was on his knees when he was killed – there are mud and grass stains – and as the blood flowed from his throat he was flung on to his face. Then the gun was placed against the base of the skull and fired. There are burns. Two more shots were fired. They smashed out through the forehead and cheeks. Then he was turned over – by a foot, I imagine, to avoid the blood – and three more shots were fired into his face – into the area not already smashed by the bullets fired from behind. They completed the mess.'

'Why?'

'I don't know. One other thing – he'd been hit on the head before he was shot, and there were marks on the wrists and round the mouth that indicated he'd been bound and gagged. I think he was hit on the head, tied up and gagged, then put in a car and taken away – but not to the calvary, because there isn't enough blood there. He was made to undress and forced to kneel. His head was jerked back and his throat was cut, and his features demolished with a gun. Then his head and shoulders were wrapped in a blanket – there are traces of it in his hair – and he was removed to the calvary and dumped.'

As Pel put the telephone down thoughtfully, it rang again. This time it was Nosjean.

'I've found the weapon that was used to hit Matajcek,' he announced.

Pel sat up. 'What is it?'

'A spade, Patron. It has blood and hair on it. It was lying inside the stable, under some straw. I've got the photographers out and they've taken pictures. It'll have to go to Fingerprints, so can I come in now and bring it with me?'

'Do you need to come in?'

'Wouldn't mind a decent meal, Patron. There's nothing up here and it's cold. And the chickens keep wandering into the house. The old fool had let the wire come loose and there's a hole big enough to drive a bus through. They're good ones, too. Marans.'

'How do you know?'

'My father kept chickens. I know a bit about them. I've made arrangements for the Heutelets to keep an eye on the cattle. They'll have to come indoors soon, anyway. The grass is already a bit sparse and it's cold.'

'How about milking?'

'They're bullocks,' Nosjean said. 'You don't milk bullocks.' Pel detected a note of sarcasm in his tone.

'The Heutelets are going to shift the pigs to their place for the time being,' Nosjean went on. 'They say the best thing with the chickens is just to leave them to find their own food. There's plenty of grain lying around and plenty of water. I've informed the Animal Rescue people.'

'You've done well, Nosjean,' Pel said.

'Can I come in then, Patron?'

Nosjean sounded like a shorn lamb and Pel gave way. 'Yes. I wouldn't want you to catch cold and die. I'll send a relief up. Get him to look around, too. Until he arrives you can carry on.'

'What am I looking for, Patron?' Nosjean sounded as if he'd been orphaned.

'Think of drugs, for a start. It might be drugs. I'll send out a sniffer dog with your relief.'

He had no sooner put the telephone down once more when it rang yet again. This time it was Judge Brisard. He sounded nasal and thick-voiced.

'You got a cold, Judge?' Pel asked cheerfully.

'Yes,' Brisard snapped.

Pel beamed at the telephone. 'I'm sorry to hear that. Best thing for a cold is a collar of garlic round your neck and a day or two in bed.'

Brisard put on a martyred tone. 'There's too much to do,' he said, 'for me to wallow in self-sympathy. I hear we've got a second murder now.'

'Not a second *murder*,' Pel corrected. 'This is only an *attempted* murder. The man's still alive.'

'Well, there's obviously someone around up there who needs bringing in, don't you think, Inspector?'

'Yes, I do.'

'Got any suspects yet?'

'Yes. But there's no reason to bring any of them in at the moment.'

Brisard digested that one for a while. Pel could almost see his small eyes glittering as he looked for some way he could menace Pel. In the end, he appeared to decide he wasn't going to get anywhere and had better save his big guns for later.

'Right,' he said. 'I'll expect to hear from you as soon as possible.'

Pel put the telephone down and scowled at it, hoping that Brisard's cold would produce complications such as

44

bronchitis, pains in the back and, if possible, congenital leprosy, so that Judge Polverari would be put on the case. He got on well with Judge Polverari, who was small and shrunken but was still a man who enjoyed his food. The few cases Pel had worked on with Polverari had turned out to be picnics because, if nothing else, Polverari insisted on eating regularly and at a good restaurant. And, because his wife had money, he invariably insisted on Pel joining him – at his expense.

Knowing Brisard would doubtless come back later with some trivial enquiry, he decided to get out of the office. Picking up Darcy, he went to see Leguyader.

Leguyader was made in the same mould as Pel, small, dark and fierce, and they had been enemies for years and were always likely to be, because they were both efficient, dedicated and short on good temper. His laboratory was enormous, with a squad of white-coated pathologists busy at the benches.

'This tattoo mark on his right forearm,' he said. 'It looks to me as if he had it put on as a youth and spent the rest of his life trying to get it off.'

He indicated a jar in which there was a small square of skin in spirit and Pel studied it with a magnifying glass.

'Could be anything,' he said. 'What about the bullets?'

'Walther-Mathurin .38. Ballistics have sent pictures.' Leguyader passed them across. 'They'll be useful when you find the gun that did it.'

'But not until. Go on.'

'His undershirt was bought in Brussels. The store mark's on the label.'

'I didn't know there *was* a label.'

'Perhaps you didn't look hard enough.' Leguyader enjoyed baiting Pel. 'It was hidden under a crust of dried blood. But it's there all right. Vemelaers: That's the name. They might remember him, but I doubt it, because it's a supermarket and self-service. I checked. There's also a laundry mark. A new one. Like the label, it was obscured by dried blood.'

'Is it local?'

'No.' Leguyader pushed over a photograph. 'That's it. I expect you can get it checked.'

Pel frowned. 'Doesn't tell us much, does it?' he said.

'It tells us a bit.' Leguyader wore an air of triumph. 'Since most men have wives to do their laundering, I'd say your dead friend's either single or was en route somewhere. And that he had a bit of cash. Otherwise, he'd have done what most people do in hotels: Washed his underwear himself and dried it out on the radiator.'

Pel turned. 'Get it round the districts, Darcy. Fast.' He stared at Leguyader. 'What else?'

Leguyader looked smug. 'Some people would be satisfied by this time.'

'I'm greedy,' Pel snapped. 'And there *is* more. I can always tell. You're dancing about like a poodle wanting to be let out.'

Leguyader scowled and lifted up the bloodstained undershirt from the top of his table. 'Smell that,' he said coldly.

Pel sniffed. The garment had lost all the odour of the man who'd worn it and the blood on it had dried to a cardboard stiffness. But there was an acrid smell about it that Pel caught at once.

'Cigars,' Leguyader pointed out.

Pel nodded. 'Supports what Minet said,' he agreed. 'Teeth stained but not his lungs. Cigar smokers don't inhale as a rule.'

Leguyader nodded. 'Exactly. If we can identify the brand we might be able to identify *him*.'

five

Sergeant Nosjean greeted the man with the sniffer dog as if he were an angel come down from heaven to rescue him from the pit of hell.

He was cold, wet and miserable, and his shoes, trousers, even his coat were smeared with the thick mud of the farmyard with its leavening of cowdung. He felt he stank like a polecat, he was hungry and had run out of cigarettes. In addition, he knew he ought to have rung his girlfriend to try to make things up between them but, since that must obviously have fallen through completely by now, he decided that perhaps he'd better fall back that evening – provided, of course, that he lived through the day – on the only girl who ever seemed to welcome him, Odile Chenandier.

As he climbed into his car, he thought of her with warmth. She was no raving beauty and inclined to be nervous – and since Nosjean had met her during an investigation into her father, she was also inclined to have a fixation about policemen.

The path through the trees from Matajcek's farm towards the main road wound round the curve of the hill. In the distance through the haze that the rain had left behind. Nosjean could see the next rise across the valley, with another huge dark clump of woodland. Suddenly Nosjean knew he loved this corner of France, and resolved there and then to complain less, to try harder, to enjoy his work more. It was what he needed to feel fulfilled. He'd start making the effort at once. How long it would last he couldn't imagine. Not long, he suspected.

A hare shot across the path just ahead and a crow lifted from the edge of the road with an indignant raucous squawk. These woods were beautiful, he thought. Lonely, empty of human beings –

He slammed on the brakes as he saw a dark figure moving swiftly through the trees. Flinging open the door, he set off after it instinctively, brushing through the wet undergrowth that drenched his clothes. For a moment he thought he'd lost the figure ahead, then he saw it again, a ragged figure with flapping jacket and wild hair and beard. Drugs, Pel had said. This looked as much like a junkie as any he'd seen.

Then he realised that the other figure's clothes were ragged less with neglect than with age. They looked as if they'd been snatched from a scarecrow, and it suddenly dawned on him that his quarry was much older than he'd thought. For an old man, however, he could certainly move, and it was only with difficulty that Nosjean drew nearer. The man in front seemed to know every twist and turn of the woods, every small opening that gave him a clear run through the trees. Stumbling after him, despite his youth Nosjean had difficulty keeping up with him, let alone catching him.

The chase seemed to go on for ages, crashing through bushes, stumbling and slipping on steep banks. On one occasion, Nosjean went headlong down an unexpected dip to land asprawl a muddy puddle in the bottom. Picking himself up, panting, aware that his coat was ruined, he scrambled, cursing, up the other side.

When he'd decided that his lungs had given out and he was existing on something other than air, he saw what looked like an encampment ahead. There was a patched tent, and a lean-to made of wattles and branches and covered with sods. A fire was sending up a thin spiral of smoke into the air.

The wild figure in front had vanished and, suspecting a trap, Nosjean's hand went to his gun and he began to move more cautiously. Apart from a jumble of tin cans, old food, a water jar, and several empty wine bottles, the lean-to was empty. From the fire and cooking implements inside, it looked as if it were used solely for cooking.

Edging warily towards the tent, Nosjean paused before the door, wondering if, when he opened the flap, he'd get the blast of a shotgun in his face. He knew his quarry was inside because he could hear movements and heavy breathing.

Pulling out his gun, he put his hand on the flap and wrenched it back. To his surprise, there was no shotgun blast. Nothing at all. Warily, he poked his head round the canvas. At the back of the tent, cowering on a ragged bed of straw and old blankets, was a man. Nosjean stared. He'd been unable to believe that anybody could be dirtier than Matajcek or Matajcek's house, but this man was.

He was thin, but he looked incredibly old so that Nosjean couldn't understand how he'd managed to run so fast. Then he realised that all the wrinkles and creases on his face were emphasised by the black lining of dirt in them, and he wasn't as old as he looked. He had extraordinarily blue eyes, however, and his mouth widened in a gap toothed nervous smile. He was panting, his face pale and sweating, and he lifted a hand clad in a well-worn woollen glove to clutch his heaving chest.

'I wondered when you'd come,' he said.

'He says his name's Bique à Poux,' Nosjean said. 'And it certainly suits him, because that's what he is – a fleabag. My car stinks like a dungheap. I thought you might like a word with him. After all, he lives in the woods, it seems, so he might have noticed something.'

'That was good thinking,' Pel said.

'You should be careful, lad,' Darcy added. 'You'll strain yourself.'

Nosjean gave Darcy a look that was supposed to be a mixture of disdain and contempt but succeeded only in indicating dudgeon. His telephone call from Orgny had brought Pel out hot-foot to Massu's sub-station in the Mairie. He was a bit disappointed because he'd expected something worthwhile and all he'd got was some old tramp who lived rough and had done most of his life.

'What's his real name?'

'He just says Bique à Poux. Massu thinks he's German but he's not sure. Seems he moves around a lot and at the moment he's resident in our diocese. But he's been seen as far north as Sémur and as far south as Lyon. I thought you might prefer him here at Orgny; while he's hot, so to speak. It was a bit of a job to get him to come. He was quite prepared to cling to the tent pole until I sawed his arms off.'

'What's he do up there?'

Nosjean gestured at Massu.

'He's well-known,' the sergeant joined in. 'He's been around a long time. He's not quite all there and all the farmers know him. He keeps to the woods and only comes out at night. I've spotted him on the road after dark more than once when I've been driving past. He's supposed to be harmless but I don't know. The farmers seem to think so, though. He snares rabbits. They say he keeps 'em down.'

'I'll take him back when you're finished, Patron,' Nosjean said. 'That was the only way I could persuade him to come without shooting him in the leg. I promised.'

'All right,' Pel agreed. 'Better go and get something to eat.'

Pel stared after Nosjean as the door closed. 'That boy's brighter than he looks,' he said. 'One day he'll make a good detective.'

'Why not tell him, Patron?' Darcy suggested gently. 'It might encourage him.'

Pel looked as if Darcy were suggesting he should make an indecent suggestion to Nosjean. Face-to-face praise wasn't part of his stock-in-trade.

Bique à Poux was sitting on the bench in the cell. He stank to high heaven and he looked terrified. His pale face still shone with sweat and as Pel stepped closer to him, he noticed a bruise over his right eye.

'What happened?' he asked.

The old man shrank away from him and looked at Massu, then back at Pel.

'Nosjean didn't do this,' Pel said sharply to the sergeant. 'Did you?'

The policeman's big shoulders moved. 'The damn sausage-eater tried to nip off.'

Pel looked hard at Massu. 'Sausage-eater?'

'He's a German.'

'And you don't like Germans?'

'Why should I? The bastards invaded France three times in seventy years and they probably would again if we gave them a chance.'

Pel sniffed. 'Perhaps that's France's fault,' he said. 'We've never been noted for electing politicians who put country before party politics. It's over now, anyway, and *you* weren't around for any of their visits.'

'I was for the last one.' Massu grinned. 'I was a kid in Dijon.' Pel gave him a cold look and glanced at Bique à Poux. 'You're strong enough to hold ten of him,' he said. 'With one hand tied behind your back. You're too free with your fists, Massu.'

He turned to the old man. Bique à Poux watched him warily out of the corner of his eyes.

'How long have you been up near Vaucheretard?' Pel asked. Watery blue eyes flickered between him and Massu. 'The young man said he'd take me back,' Bique à Poux

51

whined. As he spoke he was clutching at his chest with his gloved hand.

'You all right?' Pel asked.

The old man nodded. He was all right, he said. Just a pain. A small pain he got occasionally, probably rheumatism. He looked at Pel. When could he go back, he asked. He didn't like being indoors, because the stuffy atmosphere gave him the grippe.

Pel tried to make himself smile reassuringly. It didn't come naturally and was hard work. 'Well, we'll get you back as soon as you've answered a few questions,' he said.

The old man's eyes rolled. 'I've nothing to tell you.'

'You never know,' Pel argued. 'For instance, how about Wednesday night? Where were you?'

'Was that the night of the murder at the calvary?'

He didn't look like a man who read newspapers a lot and Pel leaned closer. 'How did you learn about that?' he asked.

'I hear people talk.'

'How?'

'In the woods. Men pass. They're talking. I'm listening. I know what goes on.'

Pel glanced at Massu. 'Yes,' he said. 'It was the night of the murder. Where were you?'

The old man's eyes rolled again. 'I was in my tent.'

'You sure?'

'Yes. Yes, of course I'm sure.'

'Have you been on Monsieur Piot's land recently?'

The old man's head shook violently.

'It's only next door.'

'No. I didn't do it.'

'Didn't do what?'

'Steal the chickens.'

'What chickens?'

'This rash of robbed henhouses,' Massu growled. The words came like a rumble of thunder. 'I thought it might be him and asked him about it.'

'When?'

'About a week ago. I saw him on the road between Savoie St Juste and Orgny.'

Pel turned to the old man. 'So you do go occasionally towards Orgny?'

Bique à Poux nodded. 'Yes. I buy wine.'

'It's a long walk,' Pel said. 'Twenty kilometres by the road. It's only seven or eight across Monsieur Piot's land. Do you mean you *never* go across the land?'

'Of course he does,' Massu said.

'I'm conducting this enquiry,' Pel snapped. 'Keep your mouth shut.' He turned again to Bique à Poux. 'How long have you been on Matajcek's land?'

'Since the summer. That's all. I didn't do any harm.'

'Did he know you were there?'

The old man was silent and Massu's voice came in a growl. 'Of course he didn't,' he said.

'I told you to keep your mouth shut.'

'Well, *he*'ll never tell you the truth.'

'Leave me to decide that.' Pel hadn't turned his head and now he gestured at the old man.

'Where were you living before you went on to Matajcek's land?' he asked.

Bique à Poux answered nervously. He had been on the Heutelet place, he said. They had never minded. Sometimes he had helped them out. He had been there a long time and before that at Bussy-la-Fontaine, moving on to Vaucheretard when Heurion had died, because the rabbits had moved. Matajcek had never seen him.

'He didn't go far from the house,' he said. 'He was always busy there.'

'Doing what?'

'Not cleaning it, that's a fact,' Massu said.

The questioning went on for half an hour but Bique à Poux wasn't much help and Pel turned eventually to Massu. 'Get hold of Nosjean,' he said.

Nosjean looked better after a beer and sandwich at the bar down the road. It obviously pleased the old man to see him because he beamed and stood up at once, clutching his ragged jacket to him with his dirty gloved paws.

'Seems to have taken a fancy to you, Nosjean,' Pel said.

'All the waifs and strays fall for me, Patron.'

'Take him down to the police canteen in the city and get him a decent meal. He looks as if he needs one. Then take him back to where you found him. No favours though – we don't want it to come back at us. Take your time,' he added quietly. 'Try to get him to talk on the way. He might say something. Try to find out how much he prowls round the woods. Where he goes. Who he sees. It's my guess he sees a lot more than he's seen himself. I'll get Lagé out to Matajcek's place. Misset's already busy and Krauss' too slow. He's best answering the telephone.'

'That used to be my job,' Nosjean said, cheered a little.

Pel lifted an eyebrow. 'Krauss' brain's not what you'd call a precision instrument,' he agreed. 'Get going.'

Nosjean hesitated. If he didn't get some time off his love life was ruined. He cleared his throat nervously. 'I've been two nights on, Patron. *And* two days.'

Pel stared at him. 'So have I.'

'I'm due for an evening off.'

'So am I. A lot of them. But you can't have it. I promised Misset. His wife's having a baby.'

'She's always having a baby!' Nosjean looked indignant. 'She has a baby every time he takes his trousers down.'

Pel was unmoved. 'Some women are quicker at it than others,' he said.

While they'd been interviewing Bique à Poux, Sergeant Darcy had gone to Dôle to talk to Piot's secretary. Suspecting she might not see him if he asked for an appointment, instead he simply climbed into his car and headed south-east towards the Jura.

Dôle looked dreary in the rain, the Spanish renaissance houses wearing a crumbled look about them in the grey light, their façades streaming with water. Piot's factory was on the east of the town, a modern building, with tractors standing outside, and as Darcy marched in through the front door of the office wing he immediately saw a notice saying 'Marie-Claire Jacquemin'. The girl sitting at the desk in a small room with an open door alongside looked up. She was remarkably pretty even if on the hefty side. She had good legs and a jacked-up bust that wobbled as she moved, and Darcy lingered a long time over her desk, enjoying the view down the top of her dress as he stated his business.

'Mademoiselle Marie-Claire's busy just now,' he was told.

'Not too busy to see the police.'

Darcy's identification card and badge produced a change of attitude at once, and the girl became helpful immediately.

A few minutes later he was being shown into a large empty office.

'Thanks,' he said to the girl. 'If you're ever run over, just mention my name: Daniel Darcy.'

She smiled. 'My name's Danielle. Danielle Delaporte.'

Darcy put on his best smile and she stared at him like a rabbit mesmerised by a stoat.

'That's far too big a coincidence to be ignored,' he said.

Marie-Claire Jacquemin's office was well furnished. On the wall, mounted on plywood was a map, and idly Darcy crossed to it. He was surprised to find it was a map of Bussy-la-Fontaine with every field and road named. Here and there it was marked by crosses. It was clearly a xeroxed copy and it puzzled him.

While he was studying it, Marie-Claire Jacquemin entered. She was a slim woman in her early thirties, with a pale face, green eyes like a cat, wide hips and endless legs that made Darcy catch his breath.

'Just looking at your map,' he said. 'That's Bussy-la-Fontaine, isn't it?'

'Yes.' She had a brisk manner and offered him a chair and a drink, both of which he accepted with alacrity. Darcy was a great one for grabbing opportunities, and this, he felt, was an opportunity in the making.

'I thought you might be coming to see me,' she said. 'I'd heard about the murder at Bussy-la-Fontaine.'

'How?'

'From Monsieur Piot.'

'Why should he ring *you* about a murder on his land?'

She smiled. 'He didn't. He rings regularly about the factory. That's when he told me. In passing, you might say.'

Darcy gestured at the room with the glass of pernod she'd given him. 'Splendid place you've got,' he said. 'For the boss' secretary.'

She smiled at him, unmoved. 'I'm no longer the boss' secretary,' she pointed out. 'I'm the boss.'

Darcy was nonplussed. 'You mean it's *your* factory?'

She gestured. 'Not quite. But Monsieur Piot passed over the management to me.'

Darcy eyed her. 'Why did he do that?'

'Because I'd worked with him for twelve years or more and I knew the job inside out. He asked me if I could do it and I said I could. So that was that.'

'Quite a jump.'

'He's a believer in liberated women.'

'What does *he* get out of it?'

'Profits and a well-run factory, to say nothing of a total absence of worry. The place hums. He draws his dividends. I do the worrying.'

'It's still a big thing to do.'

She eyed him, her smile dying. 'What are you getting at?'

'I wondered why.'

'You wondered if I'd been in his bed a few times, is that it? And this is my reward?'

Darcy gestured, making a moué with his mouth. To his surprise, she was quite unoffended.

'Well,' she said. 'You'd be right. I was and it is.'

She had been bought off, she admitted, but though she had been in love at first, after a while it had been merely convenient and she'd done well out of it. When Piot had wanted to terminate the affaire she had agreed, but only after making a few qualifications. When the unions had objected to her new position, she had sorted the matter out.

'One or two lost their jobs,' she said coolly.

'It's surprising there wasn't a strike.'

'Not the way I fixed it.'

'You good at fixing?'

'Not bad.'

'Why did your affaire with Piot finish? Was there another woman?'

Her smile came back. 'I never saw her, but I assumed there was.'

'Why?'

'He just lost interest.'

'*I* wouldn't,' Darcy said pointedly. 'Ever go out to Bussy-la-Fontaine?'

She smiled again. 'He always takes them out to Bussy.'

'Does he now? Was there anyone before you?'

'One or two. They didn't last long. Perhaps they weren't as good as I am.'

Darcy smiled. He was rapidly becoming aware that his questions were going to be a waste of time. Despite her looks, Marie-Claire Jacquemin was a hard-headed woman and not in the least sentimental.

'*Are* you good?' he asked.

She answered him frankly. 'He often told me so.'

Darcy gestured at the map on the wall.

'Why?' he said.

'Why what?'

'Why do you have that up there?'

She shrugged. 'I was always interested in Bussy. I think of it with affection still. I had some good times there.'

Darcy looked thoughtfully at the map. 'Why isn't it framed?' he asked.

She smiled. 'It's not worth framing.'

Darcy smiled, too. 'People who keep pictures – or maps – of places for which they've got a lot of affection usually do frame them. And they don't hang them in their offices.'

'I'm not sentimental. I just liked the place.'

'In fact,' Darcy went on, 'that looks exactly like the sort of thing I've seen in contractors' on-site offices. Builders use them. Land speculators use them. Just like that. Mounted on a piece of board and hung on the wall in their offices, nice and handy so they can look at it a lot. Is that what you do?'

'Always.'

He knew she was lying. 'What do the crosses mean?' he asked.

'I don't know.'

Darcy looked again at the map. 'That's a photostat,' he said. 'What happened to the original?'

'I don't know.'

'Would Piot have it?'

'I wouldn't know that either.'

She was being frankly unhelpful now and Darcy changed direction. 'This arrangement you entered into with Piot,' he said. 'The management here in return for backing off. Bit cold-blooded wasn't it?'

'No. He knew me. He knew I'd stick to my share of the bargain and I have. And so has he.'

Darcy paused. 'Do you do that sort of thing often?' he asked.

'No. I never did it before and I've never done it since.'

'What about other men?'

She eyed him. Darcy was a good-looking man, broad-shouldered, young, virile, with flashing eyes, large white teeth and a strong chin and curling mouth.

'There haven't been any other men,' she said. Then she paused and smiled, friendly again. 'Not yet!' she ended.

To Darcy it was as good as a green light, and Darcy was good at recognising green lights. It wasn't often he made a mistake.

He left Dôle, whistling cheerfully as he drove. His route back didn't carry him anywhere near Bussy-la-Fontaine but, glancing at his watch, he decided he had plenty of time and he was never one to miss a chance to advance his career.

It was late afternoon as he neared Piot's estate, and as he approached he saw Grévy, the garde, pass him in a small blue Renault heading towards Orgny. Off on his evening visit to the bar, no doubt.

A little further along the road, tucked in the trees, was a small Diane with a man sitting behind the wheel smoking. Suspicious, Darcy drove past the end of the drive to Bussy-la-Fontaine, turned the corner at the crossroads, waited for a while, then swung round and drove back. The car had gone.

He grinned and parked his car in the trees near the end of the drive. Two hours later the little Diane returned and, as it did so, Darcy started his car and pulled out abruptly to stop in front of it, blocking the drive. The man behind the wheel of the Diane was startled and scared-looking. He was smart-moustached, middle-aged and portly, and he was also no hero and seemed to expect Darcy to drag him out of his seat and beat him up.

'Who're you?' Darcy snapped. 'What's your name?'

'Tisserand.' The word was blurted out. 'Lionel Tisserand.'

'Where from?'

'Lyon.'

'What are you doing here?'

'I'm a farm salesman. Pumps. That sort of thing. I come often. It's on my round. I sell things. You can ask.'

'Do you usually come at this time of the day?'

Tisserand's eyes flickered. 'Well-no.'

'Monsieur Piot know you've been?'

'He wasn't there.'

'Albert Grévy then?'

'Well – no. He was out. Are *you* from Grévy?'

'What if I am?'

'We did nothing.'

'Who did nothing?'

'Me and Françoise.'

Darcy grinned. 'But you'd like to, wouldn't you?' he said. 'Do you often come when Grévy's out?'

'No. Just once or twice.'

'What do you and Madame Grévy do? Talk?'

'Well, no.'

'Hold hands?'

'No. Look, nothing's happened.'

'Not yet.' Darcy smiled. 'But it will soon if it goes on much longer, won't it? Let's have your full address. Give me your papers.'

'Why?' There was a faint spark of defiance. 'Who're you?'

Darcy flashed his badge. 'Police.'

Tisserand looked worried and the defiance collapsed. 'Look, you won't mention this to Grévy, will you. There's no need. There's nothing in it.'

Darcy ignored him, took the number of his car, his name and address, and sent him on his way. Watching him drive away, he decided that Françoise Grévy must often be lonely.

The woods looked dark under the low clouds as he drove

down the winding drive. The snow had gone and his wheels threw up waves of water as he splashed through the puddles. There was no one at the house so he called at the garde's cottage. Madame Grévy answered the door. She looked pink and flustered.

'Monsieur Piot went to Paris,' she said immediately. 'He decided it was all right. Nobody told him he shouldn't.'

Darcy went along with her for a while. 'Do you have his address?' he asked.

'Of course. It's in the Sixth Arrondissement. 9, Rue Charles Pegny.'

'Does he often go to Paris?'

'Fairly regularly. He's doing a forestry course there. He hopes to take over when my husband retires.' She frowned. 'And not too soon either, for me. It'll be nice to live in a street again and have neighbours. You never see anybody from month end to month end up here – especially in the winter when my husband's out.'

'Nobody?'

'No.'

'Where's your husband now?'

'Orgny.'

'When's Monsieur Piot due back?'

'I don't know. He'll telephone to us to get the food in when he's coming. We have a cellar here. And stocks. When he comes I do the cooking for him.'

'I see. Does he always come alone?'

She gave him an old-fashioned look. 'It's none of my business.'

'It had better be.' Darcy smiled. 'I've just met Monsieur Tisserand down the lane.'

She gave him a scared look. 'There's nothing going on between us.'

Darcy beamed at her. 'But things are heading that way, aren't they?'

She looked at him sullenly. 'You'd be lonely if you were up here all the time. What do you want to know?'

'Does Piot always come here alone?'

She sniffed. 'Would you? If you had all that money?'

'Ever made a pass at you?'

'No. More's the pity.'

'Do you know who it is he brings?'

'It's always the same one. He told me she's his cousin.'

'And is she?'

'Cousins don't normally share the same bed, do they?'

'Some do. Did she?'

'I make the beds. And why not? He's a bachelor. He's entitled to what he can get.'

She had no idea of the woman's name but she'd heard Piot call her 'Nadine'. She hadn't even ever seen her properly because she always arrived wearing dark glasses and a large hat or, if it were wet, holding an umbrella. She hadn't even seen her at mealtimes because it was her job only to put the meal in the oven in the kitchen so they could serve themselves, and when she had taken it in Piot always locked the door as she left. She washed up the following morning, while the woman was still in bed.

'You're sure she's not a cousin?'

'If she is, why does he keep her so well hidden? We never get to see her.'

'Never?'

Madame Grévy's face changed. 'I have a photograph,' she said.

Darcy's heart leapt. 'How did you manage that miracle? Take it when they weren't looking?'

Madame Grévy's look was cold. 'I found it down the back of a chair once after they'd gone.'

'Can I see it?'

She disappeared to the back of the room and rummaged in a drawer. The photograph had been taken in the summer with the sun shining and the leaves on the trees. Standing in the front doorway of the house was a woman, beautiful, well-dressed with an elegance that suggested wealth and more sophistication than Orgny could provide. This was Paris, Marseilles or the Côte d'Azur.

'Nice hair-do,' Darcy commented. 'Pity you don't know more about her.'

She gave him a sharp look. 'I do know more,' she said.

The woman came from Dijon. She knew this from the labels on her coats which, when they weren't bought in Paris, had been bought there. Her car also had a Dijon number.

'Which you failed to notice, of course?'

She gave him a haughty look. 'I'm not a policeman. But I noticed it was one of the new Renaults. A big one. Not like the one my husband crashed coming home drunk from Orgny.'

'Was he drunk?'

'Of course he was.'

'Is he often drunk?'

She frowned. 'Often enough to be a nuisance,' she said. '*He's* lonely, too. That's why he goes to the bar. He'd be better retired and living in a street in Chatillon with the bar in the square at the end. Then at least I'd be able to go and get him if I wanted to.'

six

Pel went home wearily that night. It had been a bad day. For Pel most days were bad days, but some were worse than others. The spade Nosjean had brought in had no fingerprints on it except Matajcek's, there had been a confrontation with Brisard who had seemed determined to bring Pel to heel, and finally an interview with the Chief.

'I can't do my work with him breathing down my neck,' Pel complained. 'My men couldn't work with me breathing down their neck, and I can't with him.'

The Chief was a big, cheerful man who spent a lot of his time sorting out the quarrels between the volatile members of his staff, and he remained unmoved.

'You've been handling people like Brisard long enough now,' he said, 'to brush him off without even turning a hair.'

Pel frowned. There were some arguments, he felt, that couldn't be settled by discussion or even by being taken to law. The answer was a duel, otherwise they'd go on rubbing each other up the wrong way for the rest of their lives. A duel, he thought, had the finality of a full stop, and he'd enjoy shooting Brisard.

What the Chief said was right, however, and Pel shifted uneasily in his chair. 'It doesn't make it any easier, all the same,' he muttered.

In the end, the Chief promised to watch the way things were going, but Pel knew him well enough to know he'd do nothing of the sort so long as the dispute didn't grow too big.

Which was exactly what Pel did when Nosjean complained about Misset, or Misset about Krauss, or Krauss about Lagé, or Lagé about Darcy. They were all human beings and often in too close proximity for too long. And they were also often overworked, cold, tired, and longing to get their feet up in their own homes, something that sometimes seemed only too rare.

Pushing the problem of Brisard aside, they discussed what to do about the Press. Pel was nervous with a murder and an attempted murder within a few kilometres of each other, both on lonely high ground, and the murder of two policemen no more than two hundred and fifty kilometres away in St Symphorien. It was decided that a statement should be made to the Press, warning people in lonely areas not to open their doors at night to strangers, and to report any unknowns they saw on the roads or anything odd that might occur.

'I'll ask them to play it down, though,' the Chief said. 'After all, we don't want to frighten the daylights out of everybody. I think they'll co-operate.'

'I wouldn't bank on Fiabon,' Pel said darkly. '*France Dimanche* could make a fight at an infants' school sound like gang warfare.'

The Chief shrugged his big shoulders. 'I'll make it pretty clear,' he said, 'that if he doesn't follow our line, he'll never get another thing from us. He'll come to heel.'

Pel had to be satisfied with that, but he consoled himself that the detective inspector in St Etienne would be having a harder time than he was. Everybody there – the Chief, the Director of Prosecutions, the Palais de Justice, the Press, perhaps even Paris and the President of the Republic – would be bearing down on *him*. Not counting Matajcek, Pel had only one body. They had two – both policemen.

The Rue Martin-de-Noinville, where Pel lived, looked shabbier than ever and as he stared at his home he wondered why he hadn't gone into commerce. By this time he might have been driving a Merc instead of the clapped-out old Peugeot that was always letting him down, owned a house in Paris and another one in the south where he could go for the worst of the weather. He might even have had Brigitte Bardot for a wife – not so young any more, of course, but with four beautiful children, two boys, two girls – and his own private jet to get around. He shuddered. It sounded horrible.

He could hear the television even as he climbed out of the car and slammed the door. The very thought of it gave him a headache.

Madame Routy was sprawled as usual in le confort anglais, leaving for Pel only the French armchair that clutched you like an iron maiden. She looked round and gestured at the television to indicate she was just watching the end of something. Madame Routy was always just watching the end of something. The end of something with Madame Routy seemed to last from the moment she took off her apron until the moment she went to bed. Had she been able to, she would have watched the end of something from the moment she got out of bed until the moment she climbed back in; and then, if it were possible, had another television on the dressing table opposite where she laid her head to watch the end of something else.

Pel stared at her in desperation, wondering what he was going to do about it this time. Every time he returned home to find the television blaring, he swore that if it happened again he'd get rid of Madame Routy and find a new housekeeper. But he always backed away from a confrontation at the last moment.

I'm a coward, he told himself, a yellow-bellied, lily-livered coward.

While he was still silently berating himself, the door opened and a small boy entered.

'Didier!'

Madame Routy tore herself away from the television long enough to explain. 'He had to come. My sister had to go and look after her father-in-law. He's ill again.'

Pel beamed and Madame Routy gave him a dirty look because she knew that, good at domestic in-fighting as she was, she wasn't half as good as Pel and Didier Darras together. From time to time the boy turned up at Pel's house to stay, and when he did they were immediately in league against her. Even her televiewing suffered.

'Not fishing weather, I'm afraid,' Pel pointed out.

'Doesn't matter,' the boy said. 'You solving any cases just now, Monsieur Pel?'

'One or two.'

'Any murders?'

'Yes. A man got shot at Orgny.'

'When they're shot, do they scream?'

Pel didn't answer and Didier went on. 'I read about it in the paper. They said it was done with a .38.'

'Yes.'

'Probably a Walther-Mathurin. That's a police pistol, isn't it?'

'Yes.'

'There must be thousands in France.'

Pel nodded. 'That's what bothers me,' he said.

The boy paused, then, seeing Pel's worn look, spoke helpfully. 'I've got a duckshoot,' he said.

In the backgarden a device like a small roundabout with four arms had been erected. On each arm were suspended cardboard pheasants, ducks or partridges, each numbered with a score according to the size of the target.

'It works by clockwork,' Didier said.

He wound it up and the arms began to revolve slowly, carrying the birds with it. He was already a dead shot.

'Mammy bought it for me because she's always having to go away to look after Grandpappy.' He fired and a duck spun off the revolving arm. 'Why not have a go with your gun, Monsieur Pel?'

'Not likely,' Pel said. 'I'd probably hit the next door neighbour.' Come to think of it, he decided, it might not be a bad idea. The next door neighbour was a railway official, big, beefy and red-faced, and he was always round at Pel's house in summer when the doors and windows were open, complaining about the noise of the television.

He glanced towards the house. 'What's for supper?' he asked. 'Soup,' Didier said. 'Yesterday's. Followed by casserole. I think that's yesterday's too.' He handed Pel the rifle. It was small and fired suction-headed darts. 'They're not heavy enough,' he said. 'The ducks fall off as if they were swooning.' He fished in his pocket. 'I made these.'

'These' were darts with metal tips.

'It's a strong gun,' he said. 'Good spring. I bet it'd fire them all right.'

With a few deft shots he successfully removed every single bird from the revolving arms, then he loaded the gun and handed it to Pel. It contained one of the metal-headed darts. 'I just want to know if it'll carry,' he explained.

It did, and there was a tinkle of glass from next door.

Pel put the gun down and headed for his car. 'I think we'll eat out,' he said.

Pel arrived at the office the next morning wilting like one of last year's leaves. Madame Routy had said nothing about her wasted efforts at the oven but she'd got her own back later, and they'd had to sit through every single programme at full blast so they could neither read, nor write or even play Scrabble in the kitchen.

Darcy was waiting in the office with Krauss. Krauss was an Alsatian, big and slow and easy-going.

'He's found something,' Darcy said.

Pel waved and Krauss pulled out his notebook.

'You don't need that,' Pel said. 'You're not giving a lecture.'

Krauss managed to turn the flourish with which he opened the notebook into another flourish to put it away.

' "Vita" Laundry in Dure,' he said. 'They saw the picture of the laundry mark in the paper and rang up to say it was theirs. Man staying at the Hôtel de la Poste down the road from them. He brought laundry in and asked them if they'd do it quickly as he was moving on. He asked them to ring the hotel when it was done. When they did so, though, he wasn't there. They left a message, but he never got it.'

'Why not?'

'He never turned up again. I rang the hotel. They reported that one of their guests had left without paying his bill.'

'Name?'

'No name, patron. He just gave a room number at the laundry.'

'What about the hotel? Don't they know?'

'They say not.'

Pel scowled. 'He's supposed to fill in a form. Everybody's supposed to fill in a form. How long is it since they saw him?'

'He hasn't been seen for three nights,' Krauss said. 'They opened his room with a master key. His suitcase's still there. He could fit our description.'

'French?' Pel asked. 'Dure's en route from Mulhouse and the German border.'

Krauss shook his head. 'Belgian, they thought.'

'Don't they know *that* even?'

'They didn't seem very sure.'

'They're supposed to be sure,' Pel said. 'The law's clear on the subject. They have to check identity cards or passports.'

Krauss shrugged. 'Well, if he were a Belgian he might be a bit dim. You know Belgians.'

Pel knew. There were a thousand stories about them: 'If a Belgian threw a hand grenade at you, what would you do?'

'Take the pin out and throw it back at him.' That sort of thing.

'What else? Did they describe him?'

'Yes. Tallish, reddish hair going grey, pale eyes.'

Pel glanced at Darcy. 'Could be him,' he said. 'What about his clothes?'

'They're still there.'

Pel turned to Darcy. 'Get over there,' he said. 'And fast.'

Dure was just to the south-west of Vesoul on the tourist route to the N73 and the south. It was a busy little town full of hotels of various sizes, of which the Hôtel de la Poste was the biggest, flashy with thick glass doors with bronze handles, a chrome bar – empty at that moment – and a vast and ornate dining room. There was nobody at the reception desk, however, and Darcy pounded the bell until a young man in a black jacket appeared.

'Who're you?' Darcy demanded, aggressively because the young man was slick and looked too smart for his own good. In reply, the young man languidly moved a small plaque across the counter with one finger. It said 'Philippe Chainat, Manager'.

Darcy showed him his badge and went for him at once. 'This missing guest of yours,' he said. 'Who was it booked him in?'

Chainat had seen too much television and thought he knew how to handle the police.

The receptionist had been away for the day, he said, so he had done it. He hadn't noticed the name and the fiche d'hôtel that should have been filled in seemed to have been lost.

'More likely he didn't fill it in,' Darcy said. 'I've been into the police station here and they tell me you've been suspected of not following the law before.'

He hadn't done any such thing but it was enough to take the self-satisfied look off Chainat's facc.

'You know it's an offence not to fill in a fiche d'hôtel,' Darcy went on. 'And you're supposed to check it with his papers or his passport.'

'Well, he *must* have filled it in.' Chainat didn't like Darcy's manner, but he was less sure of himself than he had been.

Darcy placed both hands on the counter. 'So where is it?' he demanded.

'I don't know.' Chainat flapped his hands. 'Perhaps I was called to the phone and it was overlooked. He seemed honest enough, anyway.'

'Perhaps he wasn't though,' Darcy snapped. 'How do you think the police ever manage to trace people? That's what the system's for and it won't work if nobody uses it.'

Chainat decided that nobody had ever worried before and if only the bastard in Room 34 hadn't gone missing, nobody would ever have noticed.

'Did he have a car?' Darcy asked.

Chainat shrugged. 'People don't arrive here by train.'

'What sort was it?'

Chainat sniffed. He hadn't noticed it particularly. It was white, middle-sized, a family sort of car which he thought probably had a French registration, though it might have been Belgian. He hadn't looked at it much.

'You seem to go around with your eyes shut and your mind shut,' Darcy said. 'You'd better look out. I'll get the local police to pay you a call a bit more often to see you do what you're supposed to do. What sort of man was he?'

'Usual: Head. Two legs. Two arms. Both with hands on the end.'

'Don't try to be funny with me, my friend,' Darcy snapped. 'Was he well-heeled?'

'He wasn't short of funds.'

'How long had he been here?'

'A week.'

'Did you ever see him without his shirt?'

Chainat was still trying to score. 'But of course. All our guests come down to their meals stripped to the waist.'

'I've told you,' Darcy snorted. 'Don't be funny with me. I'm trying to find out if you ever saw a tattoo on his forearm.'

'He didn't show me one,' Chainat said. 'But then it's not something you do, is it, lifting your sleeve and asking "Have you seen my tattoo?" '

'You, my friend,' Darcy said darkly, 'are asking for trouble. Anybody else in this dump of yours speak to him?'

'The barman did, I suppose. He sat at the bar the night he arrived.'

'Fetch him in. Quick. Or I'll have you run in for obstructing the law.'

The barman was a thin youth with a ferrety look and a moustache that seemed to have wilted and died on his face. He remembered the visitor well enough.

'Sure I remember him,' he said. The night he had arrived he had sat drinking pernod before his meal and whisky afterwards. The following night he hadn't appeared so he had assumed he had left. He had seemed well-off.

'Well-heeled,' was the barman's expression. 'Like most Germans.'

'German!' Darcy swung round and glared at Chainat. 'You say he was German?'

The barman shrugged. 'Well, he didn't say so. After all, you don't sit down at a bar and say "I'm a German, isn't that nice," do you? Or I'm a Belgian, or a Dutchman. Americans do, of course, but they're the ones who don't need to. It's obvious what they are. They have so much money and they're twice as big as everybody else.'

Darcy turned to Chainat. 'It strikes me, my good friend,' he said with deadly emphasis, 'that you train your staff here to be sarcastic rather than efficient. I think I *will* get the local police to keep a watch on this place.'

Chainat gestured at the barman. 'Tell him what he wants,' he said nervously. 'Without frills.'

The barman shrugged.

'He was German?'

'I thought so. He had an accent and he had plenty of money, and most Germans have these days.'

'If that's how you work it out,' Darcy said, 'you need to take a course in detection. Did he smoke?'

'Yes. Cigars.'

'French ones?'

'I wouldn't know. I can only afford Gauloises.'

'Did he buy any?'

'Not from me.'

'Did he mention his name?'

'Not to me.'

'Never?'

'It's not usual – ' the barman stopped, glanced at Chainat and shook his head. 'No, he didn't mention his name.'

Darcy turned. 'Let's have a look at his room.'

'I'll get the porter to take you up,' Chainat offered.

'No, you won't,' Darcy said. 'You'll take me up yourself.'

'I'm busy.' The words came out like the bleat of a lost sheep.

'So am I,' Darcy said. 'A man's been brutally murdered – probably your guest – and, thanks to you, we don't know who he is. Get the key.'

With a sigh, Chainat produced a key and led the way up the stairs. The hotel wasn't quite what it seemed. It had been constructed from several old houses, on to which a new façade had been built, and the stairs and corridors were narrow and creaking and looked as if they should have been condemned at the time of General Boulanger.

Number 34 was on the third floor at the top of a winding stairway covered with cheap whipcord carpet. The room looked out over the ramparts of the town to where the land fell away to the river. Through the window it was possible to see the rising land of the Vosges in the distance.

Darcy stood in the entrance and sniffed, then he crossed to the wardrobe and lifted out a suit. Holding it to his nose, he sniffed loudly.

'What do you do now?' Chainat asked bitterly. 'Put your nose to the ground and follow his scent?'

Darcy ignored him and began to go through the drawers, turning things over.

'What are you looking for?'

'Cigars.'

'What's so important about cigars?'

Again Darcy ignored him and began to stuff the clothes from the wardrobe into a suitcase he found under the bed. When he'd finished, he pushed in all the loose objects from the dressing table and slammed the case shut.

'You taking them away?' Chainat asked.

'Yes.'

'Suppose he comes back?'

'Pass him on to us. He can have them back as soon as he explains a few things.' Darcy fastened the suitcase and straightened up. 'A man'll be along to fingerprint this place.'

'*I've* done nothing,' Chainat said.

'No. But perhaps our missing friend has. Lock the door. I'll take the key. And if you've got a duplicate, I'd advise you to keep it in its drawer. If our missing friend turns up, give him my name.'

Pel, Darcy and Leguyader stood in Leguyader's laboratory staring at the suitcase on his table, its contents spilled along the surface. They all knew they were the belongings of the faceless man they'd found in the woods at Orgny, but there was nothing that might identify him.

'Pity it isn't like television,' Pel said sourly, thinking of Madame Routy. 'I've noticed that, there, there's always an initial on the hairbrush, or an address somewhere.'

'Well, Patron,' Darcy pointed out. 'The suit was made in Düsseldorf. It's on the label.'

'And the underclothing in Belgium,' Pel said.

'With a tie here bought in Paris,' Leguyader added. 'Of course,' he went on, 'there are the cigars. You get the smell of stale cigar smoke as soon as you open the case.'

'I have a nose,' Pel said.

'Give me a little time,' Leguyader offered, 'and I'll tell you exactly what he smoked and where they came from. We have charts and microscope slides of every leaf under the sun.' He fished in the pocket of a grey jacket and came out with a few fragments of dry tobacco leaf in his fingers.

'You can always find this sort of thing in a smoker's pocket somewhere,' he said. 'I expect you've got Régie Française tobacco in yours. You smoke Gauloises.'

'No, I don't,' Pel said quickly.

'He's gone in for hand-rolled,' Darcy explained.

Leguyader sniffed. 'Expensive,' he said.

'Not that kind of hand-rolled. *He* rolls them.'

Leguyader gave Pel an amused look and Pel gave a bleat of explanation, as if he'd been found guilty of fraud.

'Having to roll them makes you cut down the number,' he said. 'Unless you end up with frayed nerves, which make you smoke twice as many,' Darcy pointed out. 'Mind, you get strong fingers.'

'Never mind my fingers,' Pel snapped. 'Get busy on that car! Get a description of it out. Ask if anybody's been left with one they don't know the owner of. And try in Alsace and Lorraine. They're near the German border and they smoke a lot of cigars up there.'

When they returned to the office, Nosjean was there. He looked agitated.

'What's got you?' Pel said.

'They sent him to the hospital,' Nosjean said.

'Who?'

'The old man. Bique à Poux.'

'Why?'

'Doc Minet was in the canteen, doing his yearly examination of the kitchen. He insisted on having a look at him. I'd stayed with him all the time, Patron, as you said, but Minet took me to one side and said he'd like to examine him.'

'Why?'

'He was still a bit breathless and Minet said his heartbeat was irregular – "filibrating" was the word he used, I think. He was also pale and sweating and Minet said that in a man of his age something must have triggered it off. He thought it might have been –' Darcy glanced at his notebook – 'a silent coronary.'

'What's that?'

'I don't know, Patron.' Nosjean gestured. 'But Minet got him in one of the cells and had a look at him. When he came out he said he ought to go into hospital for observation. Judge Brisard was waiting to join him for lunch and they went into a huddle and the judge agreed. You know what the judge's like: Strong on charity and welfare and love-one-another.'

Pel nodded. He knew only too well.

Nosjean seemed worried. 'They were going to give him a bath and put him to bed when I left. It'll kill the poor old devil. If they remove all that dirt, it'll be like taking away an overcoat.'

Pel grunted. 'What's his real name? Established that yet?'

He hadn't expected that Nosjean would have, but he startled Pel.

'Yes,' he said. 'The hospital found his papers in his clothes. It's Alois Eichthal.'

'German?'

'No. Comes originally from Riquewihr, Alsace.'

'Checked him?'

'Yes. There's a family still living there. Several, in fact. I rang three of them. He's related to them all. He was a clerk but his parents died and he disappeared. They haven't seen him for years. I told them he was in hospital here but they weren't having any. He gave them up and now they're giving *him* up.'

Nosjean looked troubled and Pel patted his shoulder. 'Perhaps he's better in hospital,' he consoled. 'At least he'll be looked after and live longer to enjoy his woods. Keep an eye on him, mon brave. Try to make him talk. We might need him yet and at least we'll know where he is.'

seven

Darcy had thought he'd been shown the green light by Marie-Claire Jacquemin but to his surprise he found he couldn't make any headway with her. He'd always believed he could read the come-on signs from a woman like an Indian tracker and she'd appeared to be offering him to have him join her – after a few formalities such as dinner and drinks – in her bed. But, though he'd followed up the invitation like a pig after truffles, he'd got nowhere. She'd put him off again and again, her excuses always feeble, and it had dawned on him eventually that as far as he was concerned she was nothing more than an allumeuse – a cock teaser – and that, more than likely, despite what she said, she was still carrying a torch for Piot.

It puzzled him, and he went over to Dôle again to try his charm on her secretary, Danielle Delaporte. After all, he thought, she could make a good substitute.

Danielle Delaporte was more than willing to join him for dinner and he met her in the town centre. The hotel she suggested wasn't much but, since Darcy was short on funds and pay day was a long way away, it was perhaps just as well.

In fact, the meal turned out to be better than Darcy had expected and, with her floating in a euphoria caused by a bottle of Côte de Beaune Villages and the sparkle in Darcy's eyes, he steered the conversation round to Marie-Claire Jacquemin.

'Does she still see Piot?' he asked.

She seemed surprised that he should bother to ask.

'But of course,' she said.

'I thought there was another woman he was keen on.'

She shrugged. '*She* doesn't mean a thing, whoever she is.'

'Then they're still close?'

'Of course.'

Darcy pulled a face. No wonder he couldn't get to first base. He remembered the map of Bussy-la-Fontaine hanging in Marie-Claire Jacquemin's office. Under the circumstances it made sense.

'Does she still go to his place at Bussy?' he asked.

Danielle smiled. 'I would think these days he's more likely to come to her place in Dôle.'

'Why?'

'More comfortable. She built it last year.'

'Have you seen her with him there?'

'No. But I've heard her on the telephone making arrangements. I wasn't listening, you understand, but it seemed to be Monsieur Piot she was talking to.'

Darcy was careful not to push his questions too far. After all, his interest that evening was supposed to be in Danielle Delaporte, not Marie Claire Jacquemin. So he rubbed his foot against hers under the table and held her hand from time to time.

It was bitterly cold outside and, as she hoisted on her heavy coat, she clutched at her bosom and he saw her face go pink.

'I've broken a strap,' she said.

As she disappeared to sort things out, Darcy waited in the hall. While he was there, Tisserand, the man he'd seen waiting in the car at Bussy-la-Fontaine, came through the swing door. He looked a little careworn and had a black eye.

'Hello,' Darcy said. 'What are you doing here?'

'On my rounds.' Tisserand looked wary and ready to bolt. 'I'm staying here. I cover Chatillon, Vesoul, Dôle and Dijon.'

'What happened to the eye?'

'I had a bit of trouble.'

'With Grévy?'

'Yes. He bumped into me in Savoie St Juste. Did *you* put him on to me?'

Darcy laughed. 'Not likely. But he's no mug. He probably found out. Perhaps his wife told him.'

Tisserand looked shocked. 'She wouldn't do that.'

'She might,' Darcy said. 'Women are terrible with the drama. She probably threatened to leave him or told him you were better in bed than he is.'

Tisserand looked indignant. 'I was never in bed with her!'

Darcy shrugged. 'That wouldn't stop her saying you were, if she wanted to get at him.'

Danielle Delaporte reappeared, her bosom jacked up once more and Darcy steered her back to the apartment she shared with another girl.

'She's gone to see her mother,' she pointed out helpfully as she poured him a drink.

'Thoughtful of her,' he commented.

He put his arm round her and kissed her. As his fingers went to the back of her dress, she pushed him away.

'Don't rush it,' she said.

Darcy grinned. 'With more skill I'd have had it off before you noticed. They should teach you to undo dresses at school.'

She giggled. 'I'm not just a pushover.'

Darcy smiled. 'Of course not,' he agreed. 'But there's nothing so happy as a young, full-blooded girl suddenly introduced to the pleasures of the bed. You'll be so excited when you get revved up you'll hardly notice.'

Because Darcy was an expert, she didn't notice, and as they got their breath back he subtly steered the conversation to Marie-Claire Jacquemin again.

'That map in the office,' he said. 'Know why she has it there!'

'No.'

'What do the crosses mean?'

'I don't know.'

'Does *she* put them on?'

'No, they were on when I first saw it.'

'When was that?'

'When she first took me on. Three years ago. She'd just taken over the office from Piot.'

'And the crosses?'

'She ticks them off.'

'Why?'

'I don't know. I notice she ticks one off about every few months or so.' She stopped nibbling his ear and lifted her head to look at him. 'Did we come here to discuss her?' she asked. 'Or me?'

Leguyader was as good as his word, and he rang Pel the following morning soon after he arrived at the office.

'Handelsgold,' he said. 'A common cigar made in Germany and sold abroad – not too cheap, but not too expensive either.'

'Anything else?'

'Clothes a mixture. Some French. Some Belgian. Some German. You're looking for a Frenchman who travels in Germany and Belgium.'

'Or a German who travels in Belgium and France.'

Pel replaced the receiver and stared at the day outside. It was raining again, the water streaming down the window pane. Gloomily he rang for Darcy.

Darcy wore a smug look. Pel knew at once what he'd been up to, and since Pel had had only Madame Routy wearing out the television, the thought put him in a bad temper.

'I suppose you've been up to your old tricks again,' he said.

Darcy smiled. 'I'm going downhill faster than a greased pig, patron.'

Lagé was with him. He seemed baffled. He'd been handling the Matajcek end of the business now for twenty-four hours and he'd got nowhere. He'd even spent the whole night out at the derelict farm, searching.

'I've been over the whole place, Patron,' he said. 'So far there's only one thing I've found – dirt. He must have lived like one of his own pigs. For all I know, he shared their sty. I wouldn't be surprised.'

'What about his wife? He had one. Where's she gone?'

'I've asked around. Heutelet and Piot and Grévy. They say they last saw her six months ago. Apparently, they asked Matajcek where she'd gone but he wasn't exactly a chap to chatter much. He just told them what he told us – she'd left him. And, judging by the dirt, I'm not surprised.'

'Get on to the Press,' Pel said. 'Give them a description. Let them know we're looking for her. She might see it. It'll keep them off our necks for a bit, too.'

As Lagé left, Pel frowned. He was irritated and his mind was full of questions. He'd spent the previous night unable to read because of the television and he'd been so much on edge he'd been unable to sleep, too. And because he'd been unable to sleep, his mind had worked all night over the man at the calvary. Why dump him there, he thought. Why *there*? Why not leave him where he'd been murdered? Why undress him? Why shoot him when he was already dead?

'And why six times?' Darcy asked. 'Unless, Patron – ' he spoke slowly ' – unless it was to hide his identity. Perhaps he

82

was easily identifiable. And, if he was, perhaps *his* identity would lead to the guy who killed him.'

It was an idea. 'Any response on the teeth?'

'Not yet, Patron.'

Pel picked up the photograph Madame Grévy had found. 'No ideas yet who she might be?' he asked.

'I'm waiting for Piot, Patron,' Darcy said. 'Thought I might talk to him. But he's in Paris. Do I try him there?'

'No. Wait till he comes back.'

Darcy glanced at the photograph. 'The only thing that occurs to me about *her,*' he said, 'is that she'd be good in bed.' He glanced again at the picture. 'She appears to have a bit of cash, Patron. That's a pretty expensive-looking dress she's got on. It stands out a mile that it didn't come from Monoprix. In any case, I doubt if Piot's the sort to go in for shopgirls. That secretary of his isn't cheap either.'

'You, of course,' Pel said, 'are an expert on class.'

Darcy smiled, unabashed. 'I know it's safer to stick to your own league.'

Nosjean was suffering from conscience. He'd promised Bique à Poux that he'd take him home. It was only a shabby tent in a wood, but to the old man it was as much home as the house where Nosjean lived with his mother and father and three adoring sisters, all of whom considered him a cross between Maigret, 007 and Matt Helm.

It bothered Nosjean that he hadn't yet been able to keep his promise. He was a conscientious young man, better at his job than he realised, but troubled always by too much sensitivity, and the thought of Bique à Poux stuck in hospital when he preferred to be in the woods worried him. In the end, he climbed into his car and drove out to the Centre Hospitalieu.

The nurse in charge of the ward where he was directed shrugged when he asked about the old man. She looked like

Catherine Deneuve's younger sister, and she had a figure that showed to advantage even in her uniform. She eyed Nosjean, who was far from ill-looking, speculatively.

'He doesn't seem to respond to treatment,' she said. 'But of course, he hasn't been in long.'

Nosjean had difficulty spotting the old man. Staring round the antiseptic ward with its lockers, beds, curtains and starch-white staff, he couldn't see him anywhere. Then he saw a thin white hand waving towards him and it dawned on him that it belonged to Bique à Poux.

They'd bathed him, shaved him and washed his hair, and he was now dressed in a striped nightshirt. Doubtless they'd burned his old rags. There was nothing on his locker, no greeting card, no flowers, not even a bottle of orange juice. Lying back on the pillows, he looked frail and, now that they'd removed the dirt, much older, and without his beard, fragile.

'They took my clothes away,' he complained, and Nosjean noticed that even his voice seemed to have grown weaker.

'They'll give you new ones,' he said.

'I preferred my own.' Bique à Poux sighed. It was too hot in the hospital, he said. Airless and stuffy. He preferred the woods, where nobody bothered him. He could always see things there – birds, animals, insects. He knew all their little troubles.

Nosjean eyed him warily, wondering if the old man was pulling his leg. 'Birds?' he said. 'Animals? Insects?'

'Of course. I lived among them. Trees, too.'

'Trees?'

'Why not? They have feelings, you know, like you and me. I once heard a story about a man with special hearing who could actually hear the little scream when someone plucked a flower and the cry of agony when someone chopped down a tree.'

Nosjean stared at the old man, a little startled, then he realised that if the old man looked at things as carefully as he appeared to, perhaps Pel's suggestion that he get him to talk was a sound one.

'Ever see any people?' he asked.

'Oh, yes.' Bique à Poux smiled at last. 'Often. Poachers. A few gardes selling things that didn't belong to them. Sometimes men with other men's wives.'

'Did you see anything last Wednesday night?'

The old man's eyes flickered. 'I might have. That was a busy night.'

'Busy? In what way?'

'There were a lot of people about that night.'

'Where?'

'In the woods.'

'How many?'

'Two, I should think. That's a lot of people in the middle of the night.'

'Who were they?' Nosjean asked. 'Did you recognise any of them?'

The old man's eyes went blank and Nosjean changed the question.

'Where were you?' he asked.

'In the Bois Carré.'

'Where's that?'

'A kilometre from the shrine. It's on Matajcek's land. Where it joins Piot's land near the shrine.'

'What were you doing there?'

'Just looking round. That's all. I often look round.'

'At night?'

'There was a moon.'

'See anything?'

'No. But I heard plenty.'

'What, for instance?'

'These two men.'

'Which two men?'

'I don't know. I didn't see them. They were in the shadows.' Nosjean frowned. 'Where were they?' he asked.

'I don't know. I think they were in the Plaine. That's the big field at the bottom of the wood. It's still Vaucheretard land. I could hear their voices.'

'What were they saying?'

'I didn't hear it all. I heard one of them say something in German. Then he spoke in French and the other asked "Why?" – in French – and the other man said "I only did my duty".'

Nosjean paused. 'How did you know he spoke German?'

'I was sent to work there during the war. I spent a long time there, working on German farms. I walked all the way back from Poland in 1945 when the war was over. There was snow on the ground and I had no boots. My feet were frostbitten. I know German all right.'

Nosjean shifted his position. 'Come on, mon vieux, let's have the truth. What were you doing up there?'

Bique à Poux put on an innocent expression. 'After rabbits,' he said. 'That's all.'

'Go near the house?'

The old man's eyes flickered. 'No. Never.'

'You sure? I was hoping you might have seen someone there – someone who hit Matajcek with a spade.'

'I didn't go in that direction at all. I kept towards Bussy-la-Fontaine all the time.'

'All right. What else did you hear?'

'I heard the voices, then I went away. I thought it was safer.'

Nosjean decided the old man wasn't telling the truth, but he'd arrived at the conclusion that he was going to get little more from him.

'I'll bring you some orange juice when I come again,' he said.

'I'd rather have brandy,' Bique à Poux said.

Pel listened carefully to what Nosjean had to report.

'"I only did my duty",' he quoted. 'That doesn't sound like the sort of thing a gangster says just before he's knocked off. I think we'd better have a look round that field. Get Lagé to help you, and round up a few men from the uniformed branch. You'll probably find the gun. I'll see you up there. Massu's just telephoned to say Piot's back. I want to see him about this girlfriend of his.'

Piot was just pulling up on a tractor when Pel arrived at Bussy. He looked different in an old checked Canadienne, jeans and boots, not at all the city man he'd been when they'd first seen him.

Seeing Pel climb out of the car, he immediately dropped from the tractor and gestured towards the house. They went inside, tramping the wet sand from the courtyard after them. The hall had a misty look of damp about it but there was a roaring fire in the kitchen. Without asking, Piot disappeared and returned with glasses and a bottle.

'A touch of marc, I think, Inspector,' he smiled. 'Warms you up in this weather. Also loosens tongues, and I expect that would suit you. What do you want to know?'

Pel fished out the photograph Madame Grévy had given to Darcy and laid it on the table alongside. If Piot recognised it he showed no sign. He went on pouring the brandy without pause, passed the glasses to Pel and Darcy and sat down.

'Santé,' he said.

Pel lifted his glass, drank, then gestured at Darcy who pushed the photograph forward. Piot glanced at it and looked up with a quizzical expression.

'Do you know this woman?' Pel asked.

'Am I supposed to?'

'It was found here. Behind one of the chairs.'

'Who by?'

'Madame Grévy.'

Piot smiled. 'So she finally got around to doing some cleaning,' he said.

Pel frowned. 'Do you know her, Monsieur?'

Piot smiled and shook his head. 'Never seen her before in my life,' he said.

'Madame Grévy says she thinks she's the woman who's been seen here with you.'

Piot smiled. 'Not likely.' He glanced at the photograph. 'Mind, she's not bad, that one. Did you ever see such legs?'

'Madame Grévy said she found it down the back of one of the chairs after you'd gone back to Paris. You'd had a woman here.'

Piot smiled. 'Perhaps I did. But not this one. Perhaps it belongs to some English friends of mine. I lent them the house last summer. She looks as if she could be English. Some of those English girls – ' He saw Pel's eyes still on him, flat and blank as a snake's. 'The only girl who ever came here, Inspector,' he insisted, 'was my secretary. We had an arrangement. I told you. But it's over now.'

Pel's eyes were unwavering. 'Nobody else?' he asked.

'My cousin perhaps. And that's not her. And I'm afraid you can't contact her, either. She's been in the States for some time. Louisiana. There's a lot of French spoken there and some French people still have relatives there.'

'Name, Monsieur?'

'Moncey. Madame Moncey. She's a businesswoman. She runs a children's clothing firm. They design and make baby clothes. She's pretty good at it, too. Quite a head for business.'

'You seem to like that sort,' Darcy commented.

Piot smiled and shrugged. 'That would be normal, wouldn't it? I know a man in Marseilles who's had three wives. They all look alike – blonde, busy, and as over-decorated as a Second Empire sideboard. I can't imagine why he bothers to change them. But if you like one type, I suppose you go on liking one type. I'm not a male chauvinist pig, Inspector, who believes women should be seen and not heard, and that they should function only in the kitchen and in bed. I admire capable women. My secretary was exceedingly capable. So is my cousin. You can always ring up her firm to check what I say. I can give you the number. They'll also tell you she's in America. I'm not lying.'

'Madame Grévy thinks the woman she saw wasn't your cousin.'

'Why does she think that?'

'Because she shared your bed.'

'My cousin is thirty-two and divorced. She is also very attractive. In fact, we're third cousins, so I see no harm in taking her to bed.' Piot paused. 'I think I shall have to get rid of Madame Grévy if she makes a habit of gossiping about me. Which would be a pity, because her husband is very good at his job.'

Pel suspected that Piot's light-hearted banter was all put on and that he was carefully picking his way through the questions. 'This cousin of yours, Monsieur,' he said. 'What's her first name?'

'Clothilde.'

'Madame Grévy said you called her "Nadine".'

Piot smiled. 'Why not? She had a Russian grandmother. She escaped from Vladivostok during the revolution and settled in Paris. She even likes to use her Russian background as part of her stock-in-trade. Moody. Mercurial. Sad. All those steppes. That sort of thing. I often tease her and call her Nadine or Nadya or Anastasia – any Russian name I can think of.' Piot simled. 'It's really very simple, don't you think?'

During the afternoon it started to rain. Pel and Darcy stopped at St Seine l'Abbaye for a meal. It was cold and cheerless and the meal was indifferent.

'I don't know what French cooking's coming to,' Pel complained.

'I'm told it's even worse in Paris,' Darcy said. 'Now that the Americans have taken over. All hot dogs. You know what they're like: It isn't a meal unless it's between two pieces of bread. He paused. 'What did you make of this cousin, Chief?'

Pel shrugged. 'I've no doubt he's got one. I've no doubt also that he's had her in bed. And, finally, I've no doubt she's in America. He's far too astute to tell us something we could find out was wrong. But I think he was lying all the same. You'd better check her. You have the telephone number. And while you're at it, check *him*.'

At the Hôtel de Police, Nosjean was tapping a typewriter, slowly with two fingers, because like most policemen he'd never learned to type. As Pel passed him into his office, he rose and followed. He was still cold and tired and his clothes were soaked.

'You look like a drowned rat,' Pel said.

'I feel like one, Chief,' Nosjean said. 'That rain! Mon dieu! Comme une vache qui pisse! If I'd stood with my mouth open in it I'd have drowned. We went through that field with a fine-toothed comb. We found no weapon. We also checked all the hedges in case it had been thrown away. There was nothing.' He paused. 'There was one patch that looked as though it might have been soaked with blood, though, but I can't be certain because it's been raining for days, you'll remember, Patron. However, I took soil samples and passed them on to Leguyader. He'll soon tell us.'

'Let's hope so,' Pel commented.

'Misset was up there,' Nosjean went on. 'He's had a report about that tyre print he found. It's what we thought, a Michelin ZX 145-15 – a perfectly ordinary part-worn tyre, with nothing to make it different from all the others except a chip out of the tread. As though it's been cut by a stone.'

'So to identify it we first have to find the car that carries it?'

'Afraid so, Patron.'

'And since there must be several million cars in France,' Pel said bitterly, 'four hundred thousand in Burgundy probably, that's quite a job. We can hardly set up barriers and stop 'em all.'

'It would be a small car, Patron,' Nosjean said earnestly. 'Renault. Diane. Deux Chevaux. That would narrow it down a bit.'

Pel sighed. 'You'd better ask around the garages,' he said. 'They'll bless us. Darcy's already got one query going. I don't think we're going to get far.'

eight

The rain went on all evening. Pel played Scrabble in the kitchen with Didier Darras because Madame Routy was still in a bad temper. The neighbour had been round complaining that his greenhouse had had a pane broken and she'd had to fend him off. What was more, she still hadn't forgiven them for dodging out when she'd cooked dinner for them.

Since the television was blaring away, at Didier's prompting they started playing Scrabble at the top of their voices, betting matches on each score. As it grew riotous, in retaliation Madame Routy turned up the television. Inevitably, they started shouting louder and louder until, in the end, the man from next door arrived to complain.

'And him a policeman, too,' he said to Madame Routy while Pel hid in the kitchen, pretending to be out.

Misset was at home with his wife, listening to her going on about their increasing family. 'Three already,' she announced. 'My mother says you ought to be more careful.'

'Your mother has never had the experience of being a man and in bed with a beautiful woman like you,' Misset said gallantly, and his wife's nagging changed to a beam of pleasure.

Lagé was at the hospital, keeping an eye on Matajcek. Normally he was at home with his wife. He made model aeroplanes and his wife and son helped him. Krauss was asleep. He put the television on the minute he arrived home and promptly closed his eyes, while his wife went across the road to where her daughter lived, and spent the evening there.

Nosjean had spent the evening with Odile Chenandier. She lived in a little flat over a shop in the Rue Bossuet. Whenever Nosjean was feeling low and put upon, or when his girl-friend had thrown him over – which seemed to happen with great regularity – Nosjean went to see her. She remained as shy as she'd been when he'd first met her, but he had a feeling that he was bringing her out of herself. To the sensitive Nosjean this was a triumph, and her delight when he arrived always made him feel two metres tall.

She made him coffee and they went for a walk under the trees in the Place Wilson. On the way back, he leaned towards her to kiss her. Immediately she turned her head away.

It was disappointing because, since Nosjean had put off asking Catherine Deneuve's younger sister for a date when she was off-duty, he felt frustrated and virile as a bull, and he went home with steam coming out of his ears, wondering if he smelled.

Darcy spent an uncomplicated evening with his girlfriend, Josephine-Heloïse Aymé, and now, at five a.m. the next morning he was lying awake. Alongside him, Josephine-Heloïse Aymé was making soft little snuffling noises that were as well-bred as she was. She came from Normandy and still had in her some of the beserker Scandinavian blood that had peopled the province hundreds of years ago. It made their evenings together warm, passionate and at times somewhat gymnastic.

At that moment, however, Darcy's mind was less on Josephine-Heloïse Aymé than on Marie-Claire Jacquemin. Recalling the map in her office, he remembered something that he'd passed over at the time without thinking much about it. There were words on it, written in a German hand. *'Hier'* and *'Die beste Möglichkeit'*, and, remembering the miles he'd tramped across Bussy-la-Fontaine since the enquiry had begun, it suddenly dawned on him that the crosses on the map matched the places where Piot had turned the earth over with his digger. It suddenly seemed important and he began to climb out of bed.

The girl stirred.

'Where are you going?' she asked sleepily.

'I've got a job to do.'

'Now?' She snapped into alertness like a startled deer. 'First thing in the morning?'

'I have to,' Darcy said. 'I've got to see this dame.'

'Which dame?'

His words triggered off an explosion of anger, and for a while he listened to the tirade, gesturing one-handed as he attempted to dress and protest at the same time.

'She's involved in this business at Bussy-la-Fontaine,' he explained.

As he moved to the next room, she followed him. She was small with red-brown Norman hair and a high white forehead, and her temper was working up to full throttle.

'I'm a cop,' Darcy said. 'It's my job. I've just thought of something.'

'I'll bet you have!'

Complaining all the time, she followed him about the room as he collected his belongings. Listening stoically, he pulled his tie straight and put on his jacket, but his explanation only produced another tirade which grew shriller and angrier as he moved towards the door. As she reached for the metal breadbasket which stood empty on the sideboard, he began to run.

Outside, his back to the door, he heard the breadbasket rattle against the panels and stood listening intently for a minute as the sound of anger died away. His mouth widened into a grin, and he stared at the closed door with the crafty grin of a fox interrupted in its maraudings.

Picking up his car from the street outside, he drove towards Dôle. It was a clear day for a change, with the cloud breaking up, so that the soggy fields and the clumps of woodland stood out in sharp contrast.

The journey proved a dead loss. Marie-Claire Jacquemin was in Paris at a conference.

'She goes once a month,' Danielle Delaporte said. 'This is the day.'

She was doing some filing in Marie-Claire Jacquemin's office and she perked up considerably at Darcy's appearance.

He indicated the map on the wall.

'That map,' he said. 'Are there any other copies?'

'Yes. Probably a dozen. We had them done on the copier.'

Darcy frowned. 'Why that many?'

'Monsieur Piot asks for them occasionally.'

'Why?'

'He says they get dirty and torn.'

'How?'

'He uses them, I think. I don't know what for.'

'Can *I* have a copy?'

Darcy drove back in a detour towards Orgny. Since Dôle had produced nothing, perhaps Orgny would. As he climbed, occasionally he saw a hare in the fields, and he drove with the window open, sniffing the cold fresh air and trying not to think of Joséphine-Heloïse Aymé. That was the worst of women, he felt. There were too many of them.

As he turned into the long drive down to Bussy-la-Fontaine he almost ran into Grévy, the garde. He was driving the digger and, pulling it to one side, he waited for Darcy to pass.

Darcy stopped, however, and climbed out of his car.

'The boss awake yet?' he asked.

'Yes.' Grévy's large impassive face stared down at him. 'He gets up early, like me.'

'What are you up to?'

'Building a dam. Down behind the Bois Carré.'

'*Another* dam?'

Grévy's big shoulders moved. He had a gift of answering without speaking.

'I thought the boss did all the digging,' Darcy went on.

'I do a bit, too,' Grévy said. 'It was my idea that we bought our own digger. It's a Poclain. Previously, everything up here was done by contractors. Monsieur Heurion understood things, but he wasn't a practical man.'

'And Piot is?'

Again there was that slight movement of the shoulders that meant either yes or no.

'How do you know where to dig?'

The shoulders moved again. 'He marks the map.'

'*How?*'

'How else but with a cross?'

'And when you've dug it up, you tick it off?'

'Yes.'

'Does he then telephone his works at Dôle and tell Mademoiselle Jacquemin to cross it off on her map, too?'

'Has she got a map?' Grévy's face was blank.

'In her office,' Darcy said. 'Hanging up. It's covered with crosses, and some of them are ticked off.'

Grévy shrugged. 'I wouldn't know,' he said.

'Does he telephone her?'

'Sometimes.'

'Still?'

'Why not? He's still her boss. The telephone comes through my place so we can answer it when he's away. Sometimes, when we've forgotten to put it through to the house, I've picked it up and heard him.'

'I thought they'd broken with each other.'

Grévy's shoulders moved again. Yes or no. He wasn't saying.

'Do you think they still see each other?'

Once more, yes or no. Darcy knew he wasn't going to get a straight answer.

He waved and went back to his car. The digger's engine roared and it lumbered past him. At first Darcy thought it was going to crush the wing of his car but Grévy knew exactly what he was doing and it rumbled past at no mean speed, missing by a centimetre or two.

Darcy stared after him. Grévy was an enigmatic man. Was it just through being alone so much? Or did he have secrets? Did he know more about Piot's business than he allowed? He'd persuaded Piot to buy the digger. Was he somehow involved, too?

Darcy lit his first cigarette of the day and, climbing back into the car, drove down towards the house. The sun had just come up through the trees and he knew it was almost too early to call on people. But at this time of the morning he felt he had an advantage.

Madame Grévy was at a table outside her back door trimming vegetables, in her coat. She looked up, saw it was Darcy, frowned and went on with her work.

Darcy came up behind her and slapped her backside. She whirled at once.

'Take your hands off me, Monsieur! My backside isn't free pasturage for the hands of such as you! If my husband knew –'

'He'd probably black my eye,' Darcy said. 'Like he did Lionel Tisserand's.'

She flushed and frowned. 'There was no need for him to do that,' she said sullenly. 'There was no harm in him. He was lonely like me. It's a lonely beat he has. He just liked to talk. I thought my husband liked him, too.'

'He doesn't now,' Darcy said. 'When did you marry him?'

'1946. He was twenty-nine then and I was nineteen.'

'You must have been quite a girl.'

She frowned. 'I was never "quite a girl",' she said angrily. 'I never even had a youth. I was a child when the war started and thirteen when the Germans came. When it was over I was an adult, and soon afterwards a mother with children. Now I'm a grandmother.'

The outburst had taken Darcy by surprise. He changed the subject. 'Do you come from round here?'

'Orgny.'

'Is that where you met your husband?'

'No. I met him in Chaumont. He was working in the factory there. So was I. I moved there after the war.'

'And went to work at the factory?'

'Not at first. I was ill for some time. The effects of the war. I stayed with friends for several months. Then I went to work. My husband had also just started. He was there until he found his health was suffering. It came from being a prisoner of war.'

Darcy lit a fresh cigarette. He offered the packet to Madame Grévy. She accepted one without a word and went on working over the vegetables with it between her lips.

He gestured at the vegetables. 'They look good,' he said. 'I always say good vegetables make a good meal. So long as they're properly trimmed, and that's a sharp-looking knife you've got there.'

She stared at the knife dully. 'I wouldn't mind sticking it in you' she said.

He laughed and headed for the house. Piot was drinking coffee as he sat at the kitchen table, reading the previous day's *Bien Public*. Darcy produced the map he'd got from Dôle.

Piot stared at it calmly. 'Where did you get that?' he asked.

'Never mind where it came from,' Darcy said. 'Have you got one like it?'

'Yes.'

'What do the crosses represent?'

'I don't know.'

'Why are they ticked off?'

'I thought they were good places to dig. Dams. Road. That sort of thing.'

Darcy jabbed a finger at the map. 'That one's on high ground. Not exactly a good catchment area. What's it for?'

For the first time, Piot looked a little confused and Darcy pressed home his advantage.

'Speak German?'

'A bit.'

'Know what "Möglichkeit" means?'

'No.'

'I'll tell you. It means "possibility". Somebody wrote it on the original map. *"Die beste Möglichkeit"*. The best possibility. Who wrote that, do you think?'

Piot had regained control of his emotions. 'A German, I expect.'

'Why should a German have a map of Bossy-la-Fontaine?'

Piot shrugged. 'Well, they were all round here during the war.'

'Where did the map come from? Originally?'

'From a book. I bought some old ones from Baron de Mougy. I have a second-hand bookshop in Dijon. The students from the university use it. It brings a profit.'

'You're a great one for profits, aren't you?'

'I'd be a fool if I weren't.'

'Are they always honest profits?'

Piot's eyes narrowed. 'What do you mean?'

'Have a guess.'

Piot stared at Darcy for a while, then he smiled. 'I have a reputation for sharp practice,' he admitted.

'A fair one?'

'Not really. I'm not a crook, if that's what you want to know. I'm just quick off the mark where there's money to be made.'

Darcy paused and lit a cigarette. He offered the packet to Piot, who took one too.

As Darcy held up a match, he looked up at Piot. 'Ever visited the Château de Mougy at Ste Monique?' he asked.

'Yes. On business.'

Darcy paused and smiled. 'Ever heard of the Baron's silver plate? It was worth a fortune and it was looted during the war. It's supposed to be still around.'

'Yes.' Piot nodded. 'I've heard of it. Everybody has.'

'Ever found any of it?'

'No.'

'Hoping to?'

'That's not why I'm digging.'

Darcy frowned. 'Why did Grévy persuade you to buy a Poclain?'

Piot smiled. 'Perhaps because he was sick of using his own muscles.'

'And why does your secretary have a map like that hanging in her office?'

'Perhaps because she's fond of the place. She always was. She's a sentimental type.'

Darcy frowned. 'I'd say she was a most *un*sentimental type.'

Piot shrugged. 'You can't judge women by appearances. Sometimes the toughest bargainers are terribly sentimental.'

Darcy saw he was getting nowhere and he took his leave. It just wasn't his day because, stopping at St Seine l'Abbaye on the way back to the city to try to put things right over the telephone with Joséphine-Heloïse Aymé, all he got for his trouble was an earful of insult, a threat of suicide and promises to set her brothers on to him.

The morning conference in Pel's office was hardly a riot of enthusiasm. The man found at the calvary was still unidentified and Matajcek was still unconscious and likely to be for some time, while a bored Lagé was still waiting outside his door in case his attack had had some sort of revenge motive and there might be another attempt on him.

By this time, the Chief and the Proc were beginning to grow a little hot under the collar. A murder and an attempted murder within a kilometre or two of each other and neither throwing up any helpful clues was enough to stir the department to its foundation. Moreover, Judge Brisard was after Pel, his temper not improved by a streaming nose and a headache.

Apart from a few small leads, progress could hardly be called wildly encouraging and, as everybody disappeared to the sergeants' room, Pel sat staring bitterly at his blotter. The pattern was missing. Everything had a pattern and this business hadn't. There seemed no connection between Matajcek and the man at the calvary.

In his frustration, he set about the whole of his team, particularly Nosjean who seemed to have been specially designed by the Almighty as a victim.

'What's wrong with him?' Nosjean bleated.

Darcy shrugged. 'Probably going through the change of life,' he said.

His love life in ruins – as it always was whenever anything came up that took time – Nosjean took solace in visiting Bique à Poux. The medicine bottles filled with cheap cognac he carried bit into his wages and he knew that if there were one thing he'd never get back on expenses it was the cost of bribes of that sort, but he had a feeling that somehow it would pay off in the end.

By this time the old man had developed a great fondness for him – or for the cognac – and referred to him constantly as 'mon petit', which, if it might have been affectionate, was also embarrassing to say the least. Being addressed as 'little one' in front of Catherine Deneuve's younger sister hardly helped to produce an image of manly virility and charm.

Nevertheless, Nosjean was making headway. It hadn't escaped his notice that the rash of robbed hen-houses that had been reported before the murder at the calvary seemed to have subsided and he couldn't help feeling that Bique à Poux, despite his protestations of innocence, had been responsible.

'Not me,' the old man insisted. 'I wouldn't do that. I'm as honest as they come.'

'But you do visit the farms at night,' Nosjean pointed out.

'Not to steal chickens. To look. That's all. I have no family. Nobody wants me. I like to watch people. I like to watch children playing. I watch through the trees. I see the little boys kicking their balls and the little girls playing with their dolls. I watch them playing with dogs, and the teenagers going off into the woods together.' Bique à Poux gave a little snigger. 'The things they get up to!'

The damned old voyeur, Nosjean thought, wondering if he were wasting his sympathy on a pervert.

The old man's next words made him change his mind. 'They make me feel warm,' he said. 'I know it's wrong to watch when they don't know I'm there, but I don't watch for *that*. I just watch, that's all, and if that's what they get up to then I can't move, can I? It would just humiliate and embarrass them and ruin everything.'

'It might end up in a black eye for you, too,' Nosjean said.

The old man shrugged. 'It might. But I also like to see the older men and women sitting together having their drinks outside the house or watching the television in the evening. And the really old ones, older than me, sitting together holding hands when they know they haven't much longer to share their lives.'

Bique à Poux seemed to be in a sentimental mood but his next words changed Nosjean's mind again.

'Sometimes I see horrible things, too. I once saw a man beat a dog to death.'

'You should have reported it,' Nosjean said.

'How can I? I'd never be able to go on his land again. Sometimes I see mothers with too many children who lose their tempers because they're tired. That night in the Bois Carré –'

Nosjean was alert at once. 'What about that night in the Bois Carré?'

'Those two men cut his throat.'

Nosjean leaned forward. 'You saw it? You couldn't. It was dark!'

'I didn't see it. I heard it.'

'How could you hear it? A knife through flesh doesn't make a noise.'

Bique à Poux frowned. 'I know the sound of someone having his throat cut,' he said. 'The voice disappears in a gurgle. Wet. As if he's drowning. As he is. In his own blood.'

Nosjean's eyes narrowed. 'How do *you* know what a man having his throat cut sounds like?'

Bique à Poux's eyes became blank. 'I once cut a man's throat myself,' he said.

Nosjean reached for his notebook. 'When?'

'1945. He was a German. I was on the run from them. One of them was separated from the others and I got him from behind. He was trying to call for help when I used my knife. You remember the sound all your life.'

Nosjean was tingling with excitement by now. 'You were near enough to this man in the Bois Carré to hear that?'

'Yes.'

'Didn't you hear anything else?'

'Shots.'

'How many?'

'Five or six. I also heard someone say *"liebstandarte"* and *"Sturmbannführer."* '

'Those were German titles. SS titles. From the war.'

'Yes. Everybody in France at one time knew what those words meant.'

By this time Nosjean had decided that it might be a good idea to visit the old man's hideout in the woods as soon as possible.

'I'll be back,' he said. With patience – and patience was a detective's greatest virtue – he felt he might find out a great deal about what had happened in the woods that night the man at the calvary had been murdered because, by now, he was beginning to feel that Bique à Poux knew.

'Keep at him, Nosjean,' Pel said when he reported what he'd discovered. 'And go and take a look at his camp tomorrow. You might be right. You *might* find something.'

Darcy was late man that night. He spent the time checking through the reports and once more tried Joséphine-Heloïse Aymé. But he seemed to have disappeared with a hollow thud into the limbo where old lovers fade away.

Ah, well, he thought, there was always Danielle Delaporte, and picking up his coat, he headed for the street to find a glass of beer and something to eat. In the entrance hall, as he stopped to tell the sergeant at the desk where he was going in case there was an emergency, two policemen were leaning on the counter talking business with the man at the enquiry desk. It was police business. A boy in Toulon had poured petrol on his fiancée and set her on fire because he'd changed his mind about marrying her and hadn't the nerve to tell her, and that morning in the Avenue Victor Hugo a car had hit an old man on a crossing.

'Hitting somebody in the street,' Darcy said, 'that's sport. On a crossing, it's just sadism.'

He was heading for the door when the telephone rang. The sergeant on the desk answered it and gestured frantically to Darcy.

Leaning over the counter, Darcy took it standing up. He didn't recognise the voice.

'This is Georges Vallois-Dot,' it said. 'I'm the postmaster at Orgny. Is that Sergeant Darcy?'

Darcy could just remember meeting the postmaster in the garden behind the police station when he'd gone down from Bussy-la-Fontaine on the morning they'd found the corpse at the calvary.

'Yes,' he agreed slowly. 'This is Sergeant Darcy. What can I do for you?'

The voice came again, breathless and on edge. 'They said you were in. Can I see you?'

'Why not see my chief, Inspector Pel?'

'I'd rather it were you.'

'All right. When?'

'Tomorrow morning.'

'Why not now?'

The voice sounded agitated and uncertain. 'It's not that important. I'll come down in the morning. Will you be there?'

'I'll make a point of it.'

'I'll see you then.' There was another pause. 'Unless I change my mind. I might decide it's not necessary.'

The telephone clicked and the experienced Darcy stared at it. There was something in the wind, he decided, and it sounded as if Vallois-Dot wanted to tell him something worth knowing. It seemed, in fact, a much better idea to drive out to Orgny there and then and get it out of him. It was probably the break they were waiting for.

Pel was late, too. Later even than Darcy, because he'd been having a long session with the Chief.

Calling in a bar in the Rue de la Liberté for a coup de blanc, he sipped his wine and decided he couldn't face Madame Routy and the television, not even with Didier Darras to help. Buying a jeton, he rang home to say he would have to eat in the city, and, pleased at Madame Routy's furious yell that she'd already prepared his meal, he headed for the Relais St Armand where he'd bumped into Madame Faivre-Perret. Perhaps she'd be there again, he thought. The idea was pleasurable, and he stopped outside a furniture shop and adjusted his tie in the mirror of a dressing table in the window. Perhaps their chat this evening would be a little more intimate, he thought. Perhaps she might even invite him home. Pel almost blushed.

As he entered the Relais St Armand he saw her at once. She smiled and raised her hand in a little wave, and he was just about to cross to her table to exchange the time of day when a man appeared and sat down beside her, so that Pel's confident stride turned to an embarrassed shuffle that swung abruptly to starboard and deposited him at a table in a corner where he could see without being seen.

The food tasted like ashes and he drank too much wine, so that he left the restaurant knowing for certain he'd end up with indigestion and probably not sleep a wink. Popping a bismuth tablet into his mouth just in case, he headed for the Hôtel de Police before going home, to find out if there had been any messages.

The sergeant was just dealing with a nervous Englishwoman who'd been walking in the Parc de la Columbière and been frightened by an over-enthusiastic puppy.

'She wondered if it had hydrophobia,' he said indignantly as she left. 'In England they think we're cowering back all over France from rabid animals.'

There was a message to say that Judge Polverari had taken over Judge Brisard's interest in the murder at Butte-Avelan and was asking him to ring his home.

Pel beamed, his spirits lifting a little. The disappointment he'd felt at finding that Madame Faivre-Perret knew other men besides himself faded somewhat as, using the sergeant's telephone, he rang the judge's number. The judge answered with a booming laugh.

'You've got *me*, Pel,' he said. 'Judge Brisard's gone sick. You'd better come over and fill me in.'

Driving to the judge's house, Pel relayed what information they had so far over coffee and brandy, and was just on the way out when the telephone went.

Polverari answered it and held it out to Pel. 'For you.'

It was the sergeant on the desk at the Hôtel de Police. 'Sergeant Darcy's been asking for you, sir,' he said. 'Several times. I tried your home, but then I remembered Judge Polverari had rung, and I wondered if you were there. The sergeant left a number.'

Pel recognised the number as Massu's sub-station at Orgny and wondered what Darcy was up to out there at that time of the night. Darcy answered the telephone and he sounded excited.

'Patron,' he yelled. 'Thank God you've turned up! We've got another one on our hands!'

'Another what?'

'Another murder, Patron!'

Pel's heart dropped into his stomach with a thud, all the joy gone again at once. 'Where?'

'Orgny. I think we really have got a nut on our hands.'

Pel had a curious feeling of dread in his bones. 'Who is it?' he asked. 'Do we know him?'

'*I* do, Patron.' Darcy's voice sounded faintly angry. 'It's Vallois-Dot, the postmaster.'

nine

Vallois-Dot had been found by two brothers called Ponsardin returning home late to Orgny in an ancient Deux Chevaux after stacking cut timber on an estate near Savoie St Juste all day.

They had stopped because the Deux Chevaux was giving trouble and they had found that the petrol lead was broken. They had managed to shorten the lead but had no means of removing the broken end because neither of them possessed any tools beyond a knife.

'It has to come off,' the younger Ponsardin said.

'Of course, mon vieux,' his brother observed coldly. 'That's obvious.'

'We need tools.'

'That again is obvious. Unless you can get at it with your teeth.' The younger Ponsardin stared round wildly. The car was his and his brother was always contemptuous about it – despite the fact that he never hesitated to take a lift in it. His eye fell on a small blue Renault down the road. It was on the grass under the trees, barely visible in the lights of their car, and they could see there was a man in it.

'I'll go and ask him,' he said.

His brother stared at the car. 'Better you than me, mon brave,' he said. 'He's probably got a woman with him – probably, even, somebody else's woman.'

'Well, we've got to do something. And his car looks new. Perhaps he has some tools.'

'Perhaps even he has an engine.'

The younger Ponsardin ignored the insult. 'If he hasn't,' he said, 'he might give us a tow to the top of the hill. It's downhill all the way from there to Orgny.'

'What do we use for a tow rope?' his brother asked. 'Or perhaps it's your intention, mon brave, that I clutch his rear axle with one hand and your front axle with the other and swing between them with my feet on the fenders.'

The younger Ponsardin allowed himself a dirty look and set off walking. Reaching the car, he struck a match. Vallois-Dot was in the driver's seat, leaning towards the side of the car with his head at an angle, his spectacles crooked on his nose. Ponsardin didn't recognise him at first and decided he was a commercial traveller sleeping off the wine he'd had at dinner, and was worried about waking him. But at least there was nobody else in the car and he was more worried about what his brother would say if he didn't. He tapped on the glass.

The man in the car didn't move and, then, Ponsardin saw a black trickle of what looked like dried blood along his throat. Moving warily to the other side of the car, he recognised Vallois-Dot, whom he knew well, and saw that he had burn marks on his right ear, and blood on his face which had run down and round his throat as his head leaned to the left, to show in the small dried trickle on the left side of his neck that he'd seen from the other side of the car. His flesh was grey and his right eye, unlike his left, was still open, staring in mad fashion at Ponsardin.

Ponsardin's jaw dropped. 'Oh, mon dieu,' he said and set off running.

Goaded by anxiety and the fact that the murderer might still be lurking in the trees, the Ponsardin brothers had pushed the Deux Chevaux to the brow of the hill. It was a long way, but the body in the blue Renault provided the extra incentive and, jumping in, sweating profusely, they had coasted down the hill to Orgny.

Massu moved fast. As his car had swung out from in front of the Maine, he had run into Darcy's car as he'd left the post office. Vallois-Dot had not been at home and his wife had had no idea where he'd gone, and Darcy had been on the way to contact Massu to ask if he knew what it was all about. The screech of brakes had brought the two cars to an abrupt stop, but with no damage other than a broken wing lamp on Massu's Renault van.

When Pel arrived, lights had already been rigged up and Massu and Darcy were waiting for him, looking frozen.

'This one,' Darcy said, indicating the body, 'was involved in the other one – the murder at the calvary.'

Pel looked at him quickly. 'Why do you say that, mon brave?'

'Because he knew about it. He knew about it before I did.'

'He did?'

Darcy told him of his meeting with Vallois-Dot when he'd gone into Orgny to report the murder at the calvary.

'He knew about it before I got down there. I've asked Massu and he says *he* didn't tell him before they left. Neither did Weyl.'

'Perhaps he listened in on the telephone,' Pel said. 'It's a manual exchange. Was he a nosey type?'

'Judging by the way he tried to pump me, he was.'

They examined the body carefully. The Orgny postmaster had been shot through the head, and the gun appeared to have been placed in the hole of his right ear.

Pel stared at the body, frowning deeply, while Judge Polverari sniffed about nearby.

'Don't you think we ought to find a telephone?' he asked. 'And suggest to the Chief that he puts out another statement to the Press that's a lot firmer.'

'Hold it a little while, Judge,' Pel suggested. 'Let's have a talk with his wife.'

Vallois-Dot's wife was a small woman. She'd been preparing for bed when they arrived and, agitated because her husband was out late, had assumed at once that they'd arrived to tell her he'd been hurt in a road accident. Standing under the harsh light of an electric bulb in a flat glass shade, her face was strained and terrified. She and her husband had no children and she had helped him in the post office as a paid servant of the government.

'What am I going to do now?' she wailed. 'They won't allow me to stay here. I'm not qualified. I'm only the clerk. I shall have to leave the house and I've been here all my married life.'

'Had your husband any enemies?' Pel asked her.

'He wouldn't hurt a fly.'

That was something Pel had heard said of more than one murdered man and it didn't mean much.

She had no idea what her husband had been doing on the hillside where he had been found. He had set off for the warehouse at Savoie St Juste to get a few bottles of wine for a party they were to give for her mother's birthday.

'There was no sign of wine in the car,' Pel pointed out. 'So he obviously didn't go there. Did he receive any unexpected telephone calls?'

Madame Vallois-Dot dabbed at her eyes. He was always receiving calls, she said. Official ones. But she hadn't noticed any that were unofficial. She wasn't normally even in the post office except when her husband was busy, when he pressed a bell to summon her. Then, because the exchange wasn't automatic, she handled the telephone.

Pel paused to let her get her breath. 'Were there any letters he didn't let you read?' he asked.

No, she said. Her husband was a straightforward man who spent most of his spare time in the garden, chiefly making fires.

'What of?'

'Garden refuse. Cartons. Old papers. The refuse collection's not very good here. They let everything blow everywhere.' Through her grief, Madame Vallois-Dot tried hard to look important. 'You can't do that with government papers – not even in a village post office. I saw him burning a blanket the other week.'

Pel glanced at Darcy. 'When?'

'A week ago. A fortnight ago. I'm not sure.'

'Can you be more certain?'

'Well, it was soon after all that fuss up at Orgny.'

'Was it *your* blanket?'

'No, it wasn't. It was an old one. Brown. I don't have brown blankets. Mine are white. And I wash them regularly. Not like some people.' Madame Vallois-Dot sniffed. 'We have a bit of pride.'

Pel jerked her back to the line of questioning. 'This blanket,' he said. 'Did your husband say where it came from?'

'He said he'd used it in the chicken house. It was an old army one he'd found by the roadside some time ago. He used it to catch the feathers while he was plucking and cleaning the birds, and it was beginning to smell.'

Pel rubbed his nose and stared at his feet. 'What else did he do with his spare time?' he asked.

'He always behaved himself.' Madame Vallois-Dot drew herself up. 'Not like some people. Sometimes he went across to the bar in the evening or when we closed at lunch time. But not often. You can't afford to drink much on a postmaster's salary.'

'Who were his friends?'

She looked bewildered. 'Nobody special. He didn't belong to any societies and he had no special interest. Just his job and the house and garden and the chickens. And me. That's all. He was a very quiet man. They'd just be the people he met when he went in the bar, I suppose. The farmer along the street. The manager of the warehouse. Monsieur Heutelet. The landlord. Jean-Pierre Ferrier, who runs the garage. Sergeant Massu, of course, and Jean-Phillippe Weyl, his constable; the sub-station's at the back of the post office and our bit of land adjoins the yard where they park their van. The baker. Albert Grévy, from Bussy-la-Fontaine. Most of the people in the village, I'd say.'

'Monsieur Piot?'

'Yes, of course. Monsieur Piot. He often went in the bar. I never saw him with anyone else, though. He didn't go to football matches and he didn't look at other women.'

Georges Vallois-Dot appeared to have been a paragon of virtue. But there was obviously a flaw in his character somewhere for someone to want to shoot him.

'Had he been worried lately?' Pel asked.

She sighed. He hadn't been his usual self. He'd been quiet, brooding a little, but she had no idea why. Sometimes he had snapped at her, and that wasn't normal. 'He adored me,' she said. Of course, her husband wasn't really a happy man. Being a postmaster wasn't much of a job and the Vallois family had once had money. At least, she thought they had.

'He often felt his life was wasted here at Orgny,' she said. 'He felt he ought to have tried to do something else.'

What, Pel wondered. Smuggling? They weren't far from the Swiss frontier. Some other sort of illicit deal? Madame Vallois-Dot's next words made him realise it was probably nothing of the sort.

'I think he was frightened,' she said.

'What of?'

She shrugged. She didn't know, but she'd noticed he had been like this for about a fortnight.

'He rang the Hôtel de Police,' Darcy said. 'From a call box somewhere. He said he had something to tell us. Perhaps he heard something on the telephone, as he connected sombody up.'

If he had, she said, she had no idea what it was.

'What about the night of the 13th?' Pel asked. 'Do you know where he was that night?'

At first she thought he would have been watching television, but then she remembered that one night he had gone across to the bar.

'It might have been the 13th,' she agreed. He had been out late and she had been angry with him when he returned.

'That was the night of the murder at Bussy,' Pel said quietly. 'Did he say where he'd been?'

She shrugged. 'He just said he got talking and forgot the time.'

While Pel and Darcy were occupied the next day at Orgny with Doctor Minet, Leguyader and the rest of the tribe of experts, Nosjean was busy with another of his visits to the hospital.

Bique à Poux looked frailer than before and it was Nosjean's firm opinion that it was because he was having to wash and shave, keep regular hours, and above all, because he was living in the overheated atmosphere of the hospital.

'When are they going to let me out?' he wailed.

'When you're better,' Nosjean said, though privately he'd heard from Catherine Deneuve's younger sister that the old man's condition, if anything, was worse rather than improved. It was Nosjean's opinion, in fact, that authority, in the shape of Doctor Minet and Judge Brisard, ought to have had more sense. Heart or no heart, they were killing the old man by depriving him of the things he'd had most of his life – freedom, fresh air, and dirt.

'Are they keeping me here because of that murder?' Bique à Poux asked.

'Which murder?'

'The one at the calvary.'

'What do you know of that apart from what you heard in the Bois Carré?'

'Nothing.'

'Were you at the calvary before you went to the Bois Carré?' The old man's eyes dilated, then became narrow and wary. 'No.'

Nosjean eyed him. 'I think you were,' he insisted. What made him say it, he wasn't sure, but he was suddenly certain that the old man was on the point of a confession and that a little shoving would produce it.

'I was only there for a little while,' the old man said. 'Because I heard the voices in the field.'

'What were you doing there, anyway?'

'After rabbits.'

'At the cross?' Nosjean's eyebrows went up. 'I'd have thought the edge of the wood would have been a much better place. Rabbits live on the edge of fields, not deep in a wood. Especially under pine trees. Nothing grows under pine trees. Rabbit colonies don't spread there. They go where there's food. Why were you at the cross? Come on, let's have it.'

The old man shifted uneasily. 'I was waiting,' he said. 'That's all.'

'What for?'

'Nothing. Just waiting.'

'You don't "just wait" in the middle of a wood in the middle of the night for nothing.'

'I do. I often do. I just wait and listen to the sounds of the animals – the night animals. Listening to the trees. You can hear the grass growing and the buds opening in spring.'

Nosjean could well believe that this was one of the old man's gifts, but this time he felt he was lying.

'What happened afterwards?'

'I went back to my camp.'

'Do you often prowl round like that?'

'Yes. I told you. I see some funny things. I once saw Matajcek counting his money.'

'What money? He never had any money.'

'He did this time.'

'Matajcek?' This was news, because, judging by the condition of his home, Matajcek hadn't enough money to rub two centimes together.

'He did this time,' Bique à Poux insisted again. 'He had a lot.'

'How much?'

'I don't know. I couldn't count it. But he had it in piles.'

'Notes?'

'Yes. And some of them were big ones. He had it spread out under the lamp in little stacks.' Bique à Poux paused and ended with a rush. 'There was another man with him.'

'Did you know him?'

'No.'

'What was he like?'

Bique à Poux considered before answering. 'Not the sort of man I'd have fancied meeting in the woods after dark,' he said.

Nosjean drove back to the Hôtel de Police in a thoughtful mood. It was raining again and there was snow in it that smeared across the windscreen of his car.

Pel was sitting in his office with Darcy. They were both wet through and they looked tired. Pel had the cigarette roller on the desk and was concentrating on making a cigarette.

'They say you get the hang after a while,' he was saying.

'You've had it a fortnight,' Darcy pointed out. 'And they still look as if you'd picked them out of the litter bin.'

They listened to Nosjean's story with interest and Pel looked at Darcy, who shrugged.

'What do we know about this Matajcek?' he asked.

'Nothing much, chief,' Darcy said. 'Except that he came here just before the war when Hitler took over Czechoslovakia.'

Pel gestured at Nosjean. 'Check with the banks at Orgny and Savoie St Juste. See if Matajcek has an account. Then get half a dozen men from the uniformed branch and get out to Matajcek's place and take it apart. Look for disturbed earth. He might have been the sort to bury his money. Peasants don't trust banks. If there *is* money and it's a lot, I want to know where it came from. Is Lagé still near his bed?'

'Yes, Patron,' Nosjean said. 'I had a word with him after I left Bique à Poux. Matajcek's still unconscious.'

'Right. Off you go.'

Nosjean was lucky. He found out after only five minutes on the telephone that Matajcek had an account with Crédit Lyonnais at Savoie St Juste, so he drove out there at once and demanded to see the manager.

In the best tradition of bank officials, the manager was inclined to be unhelpful about private accounts, but when Nosjean produced his badge, he finally produced Matajcek's file.

'He has an account of one hundred and forty-five thousand, seven hundred and ninety-three francs,' he said. 'With a little more for interest.'

'One hundred and forty-five thousand francs!' Nosjean whistled. He couldn't imagine himself ever having one hundred and forty-five thousand francs in the bank. It was true Matajcek wasn't a man who went in for a wild life but, with half a dozen cows, half a dozen pigs and a few chickens, Nosjean couldn't see him even making a profit after he'd fed himself. He certainly hadn't spent anything on clothes because there wasn't even a wardrobe at Vaucheretard – nothing but an old coat, a hat and a pair of down-at-heel banana-yellow rubber boots by the back door.

It seemed a good idea to collect his six uniformed men and get out to the farm.

The check on the teeth of the victim found at the calvary had got them nowhere, and the general request for a check on commercial travellers occupied with the border areas had also produced nothing.

However, the sergeant at Savoie St Juste claimed to have seen a car resembling Vallois-Dot's Renault near his sub-station on the evening he'd been killed.

'It was in the square near the telephone box,' he said.

'See Vallois-Dot?' Pel asked.

'I don't know him. He wasn't in the car, though. I'm certain of that. He might have been anywhere.'

'What time was this?'

'Evening. He was supposed to be visiting the warehouse, wasn't he?'

'The warehouse closes at six,' Darcy pointed out. 'What was the time when you saw his car.'

'Nearer eight.'

'That's when he telephoned me.'

All it indicated with certainty was that Vallois-Dot, who had a government telephone at his disposal, which he'd doubtless used for his own purposes on more than one occasion, had chosen to use a public call box – and a public call box at Savoie St Juste, when he could have used the one at Orgny. Why?

'There's one thing,' Darcy said. 'Whoever did him in wouldn't know he'd been in touch with the police. He must have gone straight from the phone to meet whoever it was who killed him, up there where he was found.'

It seemed the most likely explanation, and the next day they managed to move another inch or two forward when a white Citröen answering the description of the car missing from the Hôtel de la Poste at Dure was turned up by the police at Rivière Française. It was on the side of the road deep in the undergrowth, and had apparently been there for several days because it was covered with twigs and a lot of bird droppings. The windows were tightly shut, and inside there was nothing but a strong smell of cigars.

Armed with photographs from the Fingerprint Department, Darcy shot off as soon as the report came in. The car was covered with prints that matched those of the man found by the calvary at Bussy-la-Fontaine and there were two which matched those on the steering wheel of Vallois-Dot's Renault. There were also one or two others which couldn't be identified.

The police sergeant at Rivière-Française was a small man, alert as a terrier, and he hadn't been idle.

'We checked the car number,' he said. 'It belongs to a hire car firm in Belfort.'

Since Belfort wasn't too far away, Darcy set off at once.

'Sure,' the owner of the hire car company said. 'I remember the guy who hired it. Tallish, well-built, fifty-ish, reddish-fair hair turning grey.'

'Anything else? Any distinguishing marks?'

'None I saw.'

'Ever seen him before?'

'Never.'

'No idea who he was?'

'For all I know, he was the Lion of Belfort.'

That evening, sitting opposite Pel at his desk, Darcy laid his findings in front of him.

'It was the guy we found at the calvary that hired that car,' he said. 'It must have been. But it's my guess that it was

Vallois-Dot who parked it where it was found.' He looked at Pel. 'Think it was Vallois-Dot who murdered him?'

'Doesn't fit.' Pel shook his head. 'He doesn't seem to have been the type. But I think he was around at the time.'

'There must have been two of them, Patron. You can't get up to Bussy-la-Fontaine without a car and, if our dead friend arrived at a point somewhere near the calvary in the one he hired in Belfort, then Vallois-Dot must have driven it away again after he was killed and left it by the roadside at Rivière Française. Then Vallois-Dot must have been picked up in another car by whoever was with him and driven home.'

'No wonder we thought that whoever carried the body to the Calvary was strong,' Pel said. 'There must have been two of them. Vallois-Dot and one other. I think our friend, the postmaster, was an accomplice to murder, but he got the wind up and was just about to spill the beans when he was shot.'

'And Matajcek?' Darcy said. 'Where does he fit in?'

'I don't know,' Pel said gloomily. 'Perhaps nowhere.'

ten

Orgny was only a small village and its church, dating back to the twelfth century, stood bang in the centre, grey, crumbling and ancient alongside the stream that ran through the place, which, that morning, was gun-metal grey under the iron sky.

Standing by the church gates, unobtrusive under the trees, Pel waited with Darcy for Vallois-Dot's funeral cortège to arrive. Here, he felt sure, was the answer to the pattern he was seeking. Everybody in Orgny knew everybody else. Family histories, family scandals and family fears were common property, and if the truth weren't to be found in this narrow village of narrow ideas, then it wouldn't be found anywhere.

Standing alongside him, Darcy moved his frozen feet, deciding that the corpses in the ground about him were probably warmer than he was.

'It's quiet,' he observed.

'You'd hardly expect it to sound like a riot,' Pel growled.

He shifted restlessly. Near him as he waited was the notice board announcing the times of masses, and under his feet a path which had been stirred by the feet of countless mourners and the hooves of generations of scrawny horses. It was a desolate place full of cast-iron crosses, beadwork wreaths and marble slabs supporting yellowing photographs under glass. Among the lachrymose stone angels there was a large and decorative tomb with a withered wreath, laced with faded red, white and blue ribbon, lying at its foot. He could just make out the words on the plinth between the trees – 'Fusillés par les Nazis'.

He shivered and fought off the urge to light a cigarette. About him were men and women in black, a few still arriving to shake hands silently before taking their place under the trees, and he was deep in thought when Darcy nudged him. As he looked up he saw the cortège approaching. Despite their lack of funds, Vallois-Dot's widow had seen fit to provide an impressive coffin covered with metal ornaments and a funeral car decorated with black and silver drapings. There were more black drapes round the church door, where the priest waited, an old man with a droplet on the end of his nose and huge black boots under his cassock, his robes touched with moisture. The whole village was there, and Pel recognised Heutelet, Piot, the Grévys, even Massu standing there on one side, square and dark, with his constable, watching everything, his black eyes alert, his dark visage heavy and solemn, eyeing the mourners, keeping an eye on the district he administered, ready like a sheepdog to herd them into the church if they strayed.

Darcy blew his nose and shifted restlessly. He wasn't even thinking of the funeral. He was thinking of Joséphine-Heloïse Aymé. He had a feeling he'd done himself a lot of no good leaving her side as he had. When he'd rung up a third time to make things right she'd told him to drop dead; at the very least it looked like being a large box of chocolates, roses or a gold bracelet.

He sighed and stared at the black-clad people filing past.

'They don't look very criminal, Patron,' he said. 'Just cold.'

When they got back to the office, Nosjean was busy at a typewriter and Krauss was on the telephone in the sergeants' room, occupied with ringing the towns along the German border.

Pel took a seat at his desk, frustrated, dyspeptic and certain he was dying. His cold was worse and the Chief was asking for a report. A report on the involved cases on the Butte-Avelan, he thought disgustedly, would take him days, and he felt like Tolstoy about to start on *War and Peace*. Gloomily he rolled a cigarette, watched it vanish in two puffs, and sadly, certain it was another nail in his coffin, took out a Gauloise. As the first whisps of smoke touched his lungs, he sat back and drew in another lungful. It seemed to go right down to his toes and, bursting into a violent fit of coughing, he felt better at once.

Fishing in his drawer, he took out the picture Madame Grévy had found behind the chair in Piot's house at Bussy-la-Fontaine. Who was she? Darcy's enquiries to Paris so far had produced very little.

Staring at the picture, Pel was certain it wasn't Piot's cousin. So who was it? The face stared back at him, serene, beautiful and clearly of good class. As Darcy said, this was no shop girl.

How could he check on it? Local, Madame Grévy had said. Wealthy. Poised. Name of Nadine. It wasn't much to go on. They might try all the expensive clothes shops. One or two might have seen her.

The calm, poised, confident face gazed at him. The hair was dressed high on her head, immaculate, the work of an expert, an expensive expert without doubt.

Hair! Pel sat bolt upright. Hair meant hairdressers! And expensive hairdressers meant Nanette!

Of course! Nanette! Nanette was the best hairdresser in the city and if this woman were local as Madame Grévy thought, she'd undoubtedly have had it styled there. Unless she were so wealthy she flew to Paris or Marseilles. There *were* women who were silly enough for that but, thinking about Piot and his attitude to women, Pel was certain that he'd never have much time for that sort. He didn't belong to the jet set and he suspected he wouldn't choose his girl-friends from among them.

He picked up the telephone nervously. 'Get me Madame Nanette's,' he said.

The man on the telephone paused. 'Who?'

'Madame Nanette's. The hairdressers.'

'You want me to arrange you a shampoo and set, sir?'

'Don't be funny,' Pel snapped. 'Get on with it.'

The voice that answered was soft and friendly.

'Is that Madame Faivre-Perret?' Pel asked. The voice became harsher at once. 'Madame Faivre-Perret doesn't work in the salon,' it said coldly. 'I can give you Barbara. She's free.'

'I shan't keep her long.'

'Fine. What is it you wanted. Tint? Shampoo? Or a cut?'

'I want to see Madame Faivre-Perret,' Pel snapped.

'She doesn't work in the salon, Monsieur. I just told you.'

'This is the Police Judiciaire,' Pel shouted. 'Tell her it's Inspector Pel!'

There was a long pause, then the telephone clicked and another voice came which Pel recognised at once.

'Inspector Pel!'

Pel's heart thumped. 'I'd like to see you, Madame,' he said. 'I have a query I'm making. You can probably help us.'

'Of course, Inspector. Come and have afternoon tea with me. About four. Will that be all right?'

'Yes – ' Pel's voice sounded rusty with disuse ' – that will be fine. I'll be there.'

He'd have preferred earlier, but afternoon tea sounded promising.

When Pel arrived at the house in the Rue Martin-de-Noinville, Madame Routy was cutting out a pattern in the sitting room, assisted by three neighbours, two small girls and Didier Darras.

'I didn't expect you home,' she said.

'I didn't expect to *be* home,' Pel pointed out.

He went to his room to change. The suit he was wearing was baggy at the knees, and had lapels that persisted in curling up at the ends.

Carefully selecting his very best, a dark charcoal grey that had cost him a fortune and was intended only for the Chief's parties or to meet the President of France when they finally decided to give him the Légion d'Honneur or elected him to the Academy, he examined himself in the mirror. The suit fitted well but it made him look like a Dutch Reform Church minister, and they were nothing to write home about when it came to being chic. Fishing in his wardrobe again, he brought out a light grey suit. But it had several spots on the front that made him look as though he fed from a trough. It would have to be the dark grey.

'Try this.'

He turned to see Didier standing by the wardrobe holding a pink shirt in his hand. It was brand new and still in its cellophane packet. Pel shied away like a frightened stallion.

'I can't wear that,' he said. 'It was given to me by my younger sister. Her husband runs a drapers' shop in Chatillon and she always sends her daughters-in-law nylon nightdresses for Christmas and me shirts like that. I think they're stock they can't get rid of.'

The boy studied the shirt carefully. 'It's not bad,' he said. 'Be all right with that grey suit. Adds a bit of colour.'

'Are you good at colour?' Pel asked.

'I might go in for art when I leave school. It has lots of advantages.'

'Well,' Pel agreed, 'artists always seem to have plenty of girls.' He studied the shirt again. 'What sort of tie?'

Didier crossed to the wardrobe and pulled out a navy blue tie from the rack. 'How about this?'

Studying himself in the get-up, Pel decided he knew nothing about clothes. For the first time in his life he didn't look like a neglected husband. Almost, you might say, like a successful businessman.

He took off the clothes carefully, laying them on the bed, then he washed and shaved and dressed himself again and brushed his hair.

'It's too flat,' Didier said. 'Don't brush it so hard. Just use a comb.'

Pel stared at him, awed. 'Where do you get these tips?'

'Mammy talking to Pappy. I expect that's it. I've got a girlfriend, too.'

Pel wished he had.

He did his hair as the boy suggested and had to admit that it *didn't* lie quite so flat as it normally did. It even, he noticed, had a suggestion of a wave, and he decided that the grey at his temples suited him. He'd been fighting baldness for years, hoping he might look distinguished for a short while before he finally had a dome like a billiard ball. He considered it one of the few successes of his life.

Reaching for the after-shave lotion he smeared it on fulsomely, then panicked and decided he'd put on too much so that he smelled like a whore's boudoir. Hurriedly washing it off again, he applied it again a little more cautiously. He decided he looked rather smart.

Didier accompanied him to the door. 'Who is she?' he asked.

Pel's jaw dropped. 'Who is who?'

'The girl you're going to see.'

'You're a true Frenchman, mon vieux,' Pel said dryly.

Driving carefully to the city, taking care not to rub against the doors of the old Peugeot because they always seemed to leak oil on to his clothes, he reached the Hôtel de Police around three o'clock.

He entered the office in light spirits. He felt almost cheerful. If he pushed a bit, he thought, he probably *would* feel cheerful.

It was the old spirit of Burgundy coming out in him, he decided, that strong undefeatable spirit that had made the province an independent monarchy and given it the power to challenge the King of France, the spirit from which had come its reputation for good eating, and given body to its fine wines. He was so overcome with pride, he was even singing softly to himself as he strode down the corridor.

The door of the sergeants' room came up and he pulled himself together and became silent, his face set and frowning, a good, no-nonsense Burgundian police inspector. Darcy was crouched over his notebook, his head down.

'I checked the cousin, Patron,' he said. 'Clothilde Moncey. Divorced. Thirty-two. Director of "Mes Enfants Babywear". At the moment on a promotion trip to the United States. Considered to have quite a head for business.'

'Did they know anything about Piot?' Pel asked.

'They did. They also suspect she has a boyfriend but they don't know who.'

He finished writing and looked up. Seeing Pel, his jaw dropped then his mouth widened in a grin.

'Turn round, Patron,' he urged. 'Let me drink you in.'

Pel flushed and Darcy's grin widened.

'Oh, mon dieu,' he said. 'Who is she, Patron?'

'Who is who?' Pel said coldly.

'Well, you'd hardly get yourself tarted up like that just to see Judge Brisard or the Proc.'

'I have to see somebody important,' Pel said. 'Sometimes it pays to be properly dressed.'

Darcy refused to be squashed and tossed a packet of Gauloises across. 'Better have these, Patron,' he said. 'For God's sake, don't offer her one of those fusées from that little gadget of yours. There's an art to chasing women and that's not part of it.'

Pel pushed open the door of the salon on the Rue de la Liberté with considerable trepidation. Being a bachelor, he was not experienced in such places.

As he entered, he was pleased to notice that the girl who received him gave him a cool, appraising glance. 'Perhaps you'll take a seat, Monsieur,' she suggested.

Pel sat, wishing he'd remembered to take a capsule to sweeten his breath a little. He'd intended to, but it had slipped his memory, and he remembered he'd had beer at lunch. What Madame Faivre-Perret would think of a man who breathed stale beer over her – even Amstel, which was good beer – he couldn't imagine.

A girl appeared in front of him. 'Madame's name, Monsieur?'

'Madame?'

'The lady Monsieur is waiting for?'

Pel scowled. 'I'm not waiting for a lady,' he said. 'I have an appointment with Madame Faivre-Perret.'

Her face fell. 'A thousand pardons, Monsieur. I didn't realise. You'll be Monsieur Pel, of course, of the Police Judiciaire.' She gave him a look which seemed to suggest she was surprised that the Police Judiciaire had such smartly-dressed officers. 'This way. Her room's upstairs.'

She led him, blushing, through a salon full of women sitting under hair-dryers reading magazines. As he passed, he was surprised to see they all lifted their heads and gave him interested glances. It made him feel better. Evariste Clovis Désiré Pel seemed to have come into his own. He felt two metres high and was sure he looked like a cross between Robert Redford and Jean-Paul Belmondo.

Madame Faivre-Perret's office was furnished in pale green and yellow, with a lot of filmy drapings. It was so feminine it almost made Pel blush with embarrassment. Almost as if he'd caught her without her clothes on.

Her attitude was brisk and friendly. 'Inspector! Sit down. Tea will be here in a moment. I didn't think we'd meet again so soon.'

'I thought of you at once,' Pel lied. 'Something cropped up. A photograph. I guessed she'd come here.' He stopped dead, realising he was babbling like an idiot. 'We're trying to identify someone,' he said more calmly. 'A young woman. She looks well-dressed and probably wealthy and it's believed she's from this city. It occurred to me that she probably came here to have her hair done.'

Madame Faivre-Perret smiled. 'That was highly intelligent of you, Inspector,' she said. 'If she's wealthy and comes from this area, that's more than likely. But first, here's the tea.'

The tray was brought in by a girl in a pink overall, and Pel felt almost domesticated as it was poured out for him into a flowered green china cup. Normally he drank out of a mug to save washing up, and it gave him a feeling of luxury and wealth. He decided he was wasting his life as a bachelor if this was the sort of thing that went with being married.

He nibbled at a biscuit and swallowed his tea. Fishing out the photograph, he laid it on the table. Madame Faivre-Perret picked it up and he was surprised to see her take a pair of spectacles from a drawer. They were large and elegantly-shaped but they changed her whole appearance. Since they also greatly enlarged her eyes, he could only assume they had strong lenses and it led him to wonder if she saw him as plainly as she appeared to, and whether he'd wasted his time putting on his best suit and pink shirt. Perhaps she was as blind as a bat.

She stared at the photograph and smiled at him. 'But of course I know her,' she said. 'She comes here once a week. It's Nadine de Mougy. She's the wife of Baron de Mougy.'

Was she, by God? Pel thought. He'd probably have to tread carefully in that case, because even in France, the home of democracy, baronnes could usually rustle up influence and he could well imagine landing himself in trouble.

'What do you know of her, Madame?' he asked.

Madame Faivre-Perret shrugged and Pel leaned forward. 'She seems to have a great deal, Madame,' he said. 'Good looks. Wealth. What more does she need?'

'Love.'

Pel's eyebrows rose.

'All women need love, Inspector.'

Pel began to feel uncomfortable. In his career he'd often had to listen to women, old as well as young, explaining their actions, some of them vicious and bloody, and he'd listened to more than one long lecture on a woman's need for love. It always made him feel uncomfortable. He could barely remember his mother and *she* seemed to have spent most of her time complaining about his father, while his younger sister in Chatillon spent most of her time complaining about his brother-in-law, as Madame Routy spent most of her time complaining about Pel. None of them, so far as he could recall, had ever mentioned the need for love.

'Go on, Madame,' he said stiffly.

'She married the Baron fifteen years ago. She's his second wife. He's twenty years older than she is.'

'She told you all this?'

Madame Faivre-Perret smiled. 'You'd be surprised what women talk to other women about.'

Pel frowned. Madame Routy only seemed to spend *her* time talking about television, the ironing, or the business of getting the next meal ready.

'Her father was Horatio Candas. He died two years ago. He seemed set to become a millionaire but unfortunately a heart attack rather got in the way. She told me he was ruthless enough to sell his soul for money and it seems that, in effect, he sold *her* – to the Baron.'

'An arranged marriage?'

'Not quite. But he pressed the baron's case well and she was only eighteen at the time. She accepted and regretted it almost at once.'

'I see. What else have you noticed?'

'I've noticed she has a lover.'

Pel's eyebrows rose, awed by her perception. 'How do you notice that, Madame?'

'I've seen her change. Her cheeks have become pink again. She dresses with care and for a purpose. She laughs again. It's quite obvious she's in love.'

eleven

The following day, Pel decided it might be a good idea to strike while the iron was hot and go to see the Baronne de Mougy. He'd heard of the Baron. Croix de Guerre, Légion d'Honneur, Cross of Lorraine. Bit of a cold fish, he'd heard. Just the sort to buy the affection of a young girl and lose it again just as quickly.

Since she was a baronne, he felt she, too, rated the grey suit-pink shirt routine. The shirt was still clean and he could wear it once more before putting it to wash for Madame Routy to ruin. When he went home to change, Madame Routy eyed him suspiciously.

'Have you got a woman or something?' she asked.

Pel disdained to reply, chiefly because he could never find anything biting enough to quieten Madame Routy. He had the enviable reputation of being able to reduce his staff – save perhaps Darcy – to tears, but Madame Routy was impervious. And with Madame Routy, anyway, he only managed to think up his biting comments after she'd left the room and had to mouth them to the empty air. Chiefly, he felt, he endured her because good housekeepers were hard to get and, though Madame Routy wasn't the best, she was far from being the worst.

She was still staring at him suspiciously. 'Because if you have,' she said, 'I want three months notice. A woman my age can't find another job as easily as all that. And I'd need a good reference.'

Listens to the television from breakfast time to falling asleep, Pel thought. Uses the volume control as if she were piloting a 747. Full boost. We have lift-off. Or was that rockets? Either way, it wouldn't look so hot in a reference.

On the other hand, he knew he'd never write any such thing because he'd never dare hand it to her.

It was easy enough to find the Baronne's address from the telephone book. Her apartment was in the centre of the old city, close to the Palace of the Dukes with its turrets and blue-tiled roofs and the tower of the Eglise de Notre Dame behind.

Pel was shown into a panelled room filled with Louis Quinze furniture. The Baronne was tall, languid, blonde and more beautiful even than the photograph. The de Mougys belonged to the old aristocracy, not the parvenus of the Second Empire, and she went with them. She'd have looked chic in a sack, Pel decided, and there was an ambience about her that made him feel vaguely commonplace.

'Do you always live here, Madame la Baronne?' he asked.

The luxury about him was enough to take his breath away.

She smiled, graciously condescending. 'No. We're often at the château. It's at Ste Monique. It's not a big one. Nothing like Bussy-Rabutin or Ancy-le-Franc, or the châteaux of the Loire. It's quite small, really –' probably only covering four or five hectares, Pel thought ' – so we've been able to prevent it decaying. Also, my husband was one of the first men in France to go in for the frozen food business. He's transformed eating.'

Not for the better, Pel thought, deciding he didn't like the Baron. No true Frenchman could possibly like a man who'd brought that transatlantic horror, frozen food, to France. Though, doubtless, he was a great favourite with Madame Routy.

'He used the stables,' the Baronne was saying, 'and set up freezers there. We supply Monoprix and many other stores.'

'The Baron must be a busy man,' Pel said politely.

She smiled. Very busy, she admitted. He went all over France selling their products, even to Belgium and Germany.

'And he has a manager to run the plant?' Pel asked.

She smiled again. Oh, no, she said. She attended to that.

Another of Piot's capable women, Pel thought. 'I'm investigating a murder, Madame,' he said. 'At Bussy-la-Fontaine.'

Her face became blank and wary. She'd heard of it, she said. Pel glanced about him. What he had to say seemed best said in private. Establishing that the Baron was away from home, he leaned forward. 'What I have to say, Madame,' he pointed out, 'concerns you. You and Monsieur Piot.'

Her manner changed from friendliness to hostility at once, and when Pel told her what he'd discovered about her, she sat silently for a long time, almost as if she were petrified. When she spoke, however, he realised it wasn't terror that had caused her silence.

'Yes,' she admitted slowly. 'I am that woman. I trust you'll keep the information to yourself.'

Pel frowned, affronted. 'It's not the police department's business, Madame,' he said stiffly, 'to become involved in domestic affairs. We're not involved with morals and it's no concern of mine. All I want to know is something about Monsieur Piot.'

Her manner softened. She offered him a cigarette and a cognac. He refused the cognac because he felt his stomach would never cope with it, but, having smoked nothing since getting up but his rolled confections, he accepted the cigarette with alacrity. He was already growing tired of cigarettes that either exploded in the face to singe the eyelashes or were so difficult to draw on he could feel his toes curling up as he sucked at them. When it came, however, the cigarette wasn't a Gauloise, strong and black and harsh enough to give him the coughing fit that always restored his morale, but something scented in red paper. It tasted like nothing on earth.

'I heard about his trouble, of course,' the Baronne said, sitting back. 'He telephoned me.'

'He told *you* all about it?'

'He told me a man had been found dead on his land and that he'd obviously been murdered.'

'Did he suggest any reasons?'

'He seemed baffled by it. It's such a sorry business and must be a great trial to him. Especially after what happened to his father.'

Pel's ears cocked like a spaniel after a pheasant. 'What did happen to his father, Madame?'

'Didn't you know? He was shot by the Germans.'

'In the Forest of Orgny?'

'Oh, no. On the Vercors Massif near Grenoble. It was very sad. I was just a baby, of course, but I know about that business. I understand they put out flags after the invasion and decided to defy the Germans. Unfortunately, the Germans sent in a division of troops with gliders and tanks and that was that.'

Pel *had* heard of it.

'How *did* you hear about all this, Madame?' he asked.

'My husband told me.' She gestured. 'He was a leader of the Resistance round here, of course. He was decorated by General de Gaulle. I'm told he was quite ruthless.'

Pel considered for a moment, staring at the cigarette she'd given him and wondering what on earth it could be made of. 'Your husband, Madame,' he said. 'I understand he's older than you?'

'Yes. Twenty-five years.'

'That would put him in his late fifties.'

She smiled. 'You flatter me. I'm almost forty. He's sixty-four.'

'Could you describe him?'

'I can do better than that. I can show you a portrait. What has he been up to?'

'Nothing, I hope, Madame,' Pel said slowly. 'I'm merely pursuing a line of enquiry.'

She led him into the library and gestured at a painting on the wall. It showed a tall, erect man in his forties dressed in riding clothes. He was strong-featured with a face like a hatchet. His hair, close-cropped in the manner the Resistance had favoured, was golden, Pel noticed, with reddish lights in it, though whether the red was artist's licence or not it was hard to say because there was a setting sun and a pink sky behind him. A companion portrait showed the Baronne, also in riding clothes. She must have been about eighteen at the time, ravishingly beautiful and slender as a wraith.

'They were painted when we were married,' she said.

'The Baron's wearing the Légion d'Honneur,' Pel observed.

'He was given that for his work in the Resistance. He was very proud of it.'

Pel cleared his throat. 'Did *he* know about Monsieur Piot, Madame?'

'Of course not.' She gave him a cool little smile. 'It would have been very foolish of me to allow that to happen.'

'Monsieur Piot: What did he think of the Baron?'

'Not very much.'

'But this ah – situation that had arisen between you?'

Her expression didn't change. 'It was most unfortunate.'

'Did Monsieur Piot wish to do anything about it?'

'He wanted to marry me.'

'But the Baron was in the way?'

'But, of course. But for the Baron we'd have married long since.'

'But the Baron wouldn't permit a divorce?'

'He was never asked. We knew it was useless. He was a quick-tempered man, and a fine swordsman. He represented France with sabres and pistol in the Olympic Games of 1936.'

'So that if Monsieur Piot wished to marry you, divorce wasn't the answer?'

'Hardly. My husband was a good catholic and didn't believe in it. It would never have been possible.'

Pel drew a deep breath. Suddenly his heart began to beat faster. All that nonsense about German commercial travellers and questionnaires to the police along the borders had been a sheer waste of time. The thing was staring him in the face – a crime passionel, a simple domestic issue! They'd been looking down all the wrong avenues, seeing ghosts where there weren't any, making up complicated conspiracies in Orgny where they didn't exist. There were still a few things to be cleared up, of course. For instance, why a hired car and a hotel in Dure he couldn't imagine. Perhaps that was connected with something else entirely, but at least he seemed to be making headway at last, and he could thank Madame Faivre-Perret, Didier Darras and the pink shirt for it.

'Did your husband know Monsieur Piot?' he asked. 'Personally?'

She smiled. 'Yes, of course. They were both in business in the city. They were both members of the Chamber of Commerce.'

'Did he know Georges Vallois-Dot?'

'Who?' She looked quite blank.

'Georges Vallois-Dot. The postmaster at Orgny. He's just been found murdered.'

Her eyes widened and a smile crossed her face. 'You're not suggesting my husband murdered him, surely?'

Pel wasn't. The thought was the farthest thing from his mind. Quite the opposite, in fact.

'No, Madame,' he said stiffly. 'I'm not.'

The Baronne was still smiling. 'Well, of course, he *might* have known him. We have to pass through Orgny on our way to Dijon. In fact Orgny's the first place we can post letters, and he often went off with a briefcase full of them. Business letters. Perhaps he posted them in Orgny instead of Dijon. Perhaps that's how he knew him.'

Pel was beginning to feel sure of himself. 'Your husband, Madame,' he said. 'Does he smoke?'

She smiled. 'Of course.'

'Cigars?'

'He loves them.'

'German cigars?'

'I doubt it. He's a good Frenchman. Though, he might have done. He sometimes visits Germany as I've said.'

'By which route did he go?'

'The usual way from here, I suppose. Vesoul, Mulhouse and on to Stuttgart.'

'That would be via Dure, wouldn't it?'

'Would it?' The Baronne moved her shoulders in an elegant shrug. 'I don't know the place.'

He hadn't expected she would. Dure was hardly the place to capture the imagination of someone as beautiful, expensive and sophisticated as the Baronne.

She was watching him as he fiddled with his notebook and ballpoint. 'Does all this have a bearing on your murder, Inspector?' she asked.

Indeed it did, Pel thought. 'Yes, Madame,' he said. 'I think it does. Tell me, how tall would you say your husband was?'

'He's one metre seventy-six, I think.'

'Quite tall?'

'Yes.'

'And well-built?'

'Yes.'

'Had he been wounded during the war?'

138

'Yes, he had. During the battle for Amiens. He was demobilised after the Occupation. A little influence, I suspect, because he never went to a German prison camp. It was after that he joined the Resistance.'

'This wound, Madame – ' Pel's heart was thudding ' – was it in the calf?'

She looked surprised. 'No. In the ankle. Right ankle.'

Well, Pel thought, people probably had different ideas about where the ankle ended and the calf began.

'Where exactly, Madame?'

She pointed vaguely to her leg. 'It was an old scar. I didn't make a point of examining it often.'

'Of course not. How about tattoos?'

She looked startled. 'Tattoos? I imagine he'd never have dreamed of being tattooed.'

Pel pointed to his forearm. 'About here, Madame.'

'I never saw one.'

'It was very faint. It had been erased. It could almost look like the blueness of veins.'

She looked blank. 'It's possible,' she admitted. 'We never made a fetish of examining each other's bodies. But it's possible. He served in the Navy as a boy.'

He did? Pel's heart jumped with certainty. The sailor they were looking for!

'Where is your husband now, Madame?'

She looked surprised. 'At his hotel in Paris, I imagine,' she said. 'He went there on business.'

'And the hotel, Madame?'

'Hôtel Angleterre, Rue Jacob. He always stays there. So did his father.' She gave a little smile. 'The de Mougys are creatures of habit.'

'Have you spoken to him since he went to Paris?'

She looked startled again. 'No, of course not.'

'Ah!' Pel almost smiled. The thing seemed to be sewn up. All it required was a visit to Madame Vallois-Dot to check whether she'd ever seen the Baron in the Orgny post office, then he'd see Judge Polverari that evening and Piot soon afterwards. 'You're quite sure he's in Paris, of course?'

'Of course.'

Pel pounced. 'But when did you last see him, Madame?'

She smiled. 'This morning,' she said. 'He left on the early train. I drove him to the station myself.'

twelve

Pel was deflated.

He'd done what no detective should ever do. He'd made the facts fit his own theories. Until he'd discovered the Baronne, he'd continued to assume that the murder at the calvary had been connected somehow with Orgny or the district around, but the fact that the Baron was the obstacle to Piot marrying the Baronne had made him jump to conclusions. And they'd been the wrong conclusions.

It had been a bad mistake – though, fortunately, he hadn't got as far as an accusation and made a fool of himself. But what he'd begun to feel might be a good lead had fallen flat on its face. The Baronne had borne out Piot's words that he liked intelligent women. She'd been cool and capable, and under other circumstances, Pel suspected she'd have made a hard-headed businesswoman.

He decided gloomily that he wasn't in the same league as the Baronne and Madame Faivre-Perret. The Baronne had made him feel lacking in manners, and the pink shirt had suddenly become sugar icing-coloured and hideously wrong.

There was little else to report. Leguyader's tests on the soil samples taken from the field near the Bois Carré showed blood – the same blood as that of the man found at the calvary – which seemed to suggest he'd been murdered there – but the tyre print they'd found was from a sort of tyre that was fitted to every small car in France, and the chance of finding the owner looked slim indeed.

Only Darcy's discovery of the map of Bussy-la-Fontaine at Dôle seemed to suggest a lead.

'That former secretary of Piot's,' Pel said. 'What do you make of her?'

'Beautiful,' Darcy kissed his fingertips.

'As a suspect, I mean.'

Darcy shrugged. 'Hard-headed. Enigmatic. Clever. In bed, too, I've no doubt, because she has an experienced look in her eye.'

'How do you know?'

Darcy smiled. 'I have one myself.'

Pel frowned. 'Take another look at her,' he suggested.

As Darcy left, Pel studied the notes he'd made on his blotter. Grévy, he'd written. Madame Grévy. Emile Heutelet. Bique à Poux. None of them seemed to fit somehow. Matajcek was just the type, he felt, but *he* couldn't have killed Vallois-Dot, and somehow he felt that the attack on Matajcek had nothing to do with the other case. But why didn't Madame Matajcek contact them? The information that she was being sought had been in the newspapers for days now and she must have seen it.

There was, he decided, something still missing somewhere.

Darcy set about watching Marie-Claire Jacquemin quite simply by watching Piot first.

He parked his car on the high land at Butte-Avelan just beyond Bussy-la-Fontaine where he could look down without being seen on to the road past the entrance to the drive. At six-thirty in the evening, he saw Piot's Mercedes pull out and head towards the east. Putting his car in motion, he set off after him. He hadn't a cat in hell's chance of keeping up with a Merc in a Peugeot, but there was a lot of traffic on the road that slowed Piot down and he was able to keep him in sight long enough to realise he was heading for Dôle, as he'd expected.

At Dôle, he prowled round the town until he saw the Merc parked outside a restaurant, so he halted across the road, had a word with the policeman on duty in the square who wanted to pull him in for parking, and sat watching from behind a newspaper.

At nine-thirty, Piot reappeared and, as Darcy had expected, he was accompanied by Marie-Claire Jacquemin. She was clinging to his arm, looking up at him and laughing.

They climbed into the Merc and set off out of the centre of the town. Darcy followed. On the outskirts, there was a neat white house in a tidy garden and they swung into the drive and went inside, Marie-Claire Jacquemin opening the door with a key from her handbag.

Finding a well-shadowed place under the trees, Darcy pulled up his collar and sat back to watch. It was going to be a long cold wait, he decided.

It was. He was there until next morning.

As he watched Piot drive away in the growing daylight, he decided that the ramifications of the thing were growing and, as usual, with everybody trying to hide their misdeeds, they were all lying like lunatics. Piot obviously wasn't digging dams. And Marie-Claire Jacquemin wasn't just running his works for fun, but so that he could spend his time at Bussy-la-Fontaine. Was Grévy involved too? After all, Darcy had seen him on the digger and surely Piot would never trust him with the chance of finding the loot unless he were. And where did Madame Grévy fit in?

Probably nowhere, he thought bitterly. Probably none of them did. All sorts of things appeared to have malevolent meanings until a case was cleared up, when they turned out to be quite innocent, purely coincidental or just dirty little affairs that just happened to have come to light.

It seemed to be time to find a bar for breakfast.

Marie-Claire Jacquemin was surprised to see Darcy again when he turned up at her office, and this time not half so pleased. She looked at him like a housewife at a broken-down washing machine, and he noticed also that Danielle Delaporte was no longer in the office next door.

'I don't like the police coming here to pump my employees,' Marie-Claire Jacquemin snapped.

Darcy was unmoved. 'The police have to do their work,' he said.

'I could have you turned off these premises,' she said.

Darcy smiled. 'And I, mademoiselle, could very probably have you arrested.'

'What for?'

'Conspiracy.'

She sneered. 'Conspiracy to do what?'

'To rob the Baron de Mougy.' He gestured at the wall. 'You discovered the original of that map in a book which had belonged to him and, instead of returning it to him, as you should have, or at least showing it to him, you passed it on to Paul-Edouard Piot who promptly started to dig up Bussy-la-Fontaine for the loot from the Baron's place that he felt sure was marked on it. If he were to find it, it would be stealing by finding and you would be involved.'

Her face fell.

Darcy smiled. 'I even suspect that your friend, Piot, paid court to the Baronne and got her into bed at *your* instigation. To find out what he could about it. Am I right?'

Her cheeks reddened. 'What proof have you?'

'Well, contrary to what you told me and what you tell other people, you've never broken with him.'

'Of course I have.'

'Then what was he doing in your house – and doubtless in your bed – from nine-thirty last night until seven-thirty this morning when you left for work and he went in the direction of Butte-Avelan?'

She flushed. 'You were watching?'

'I wish I could have got closer.'

'You're nothing but a damned voyeur!'

Darcy smiled. 'It's one of the pleasanter perks of police work. We often do it. Especially when the woman's as attractive as you are and we think someone's telling lies. What were you getting out of it? A cut if they found the loot?'

While Pel had been visiting the Baronne and Darcy had been watching Piot and Marie-Claire Jacquemin, Nosjean had been tearing Matajcek's farm apart. It had gone on all the previous day and well into the evening.

That morning, the men working during the night had been relieved and Nosjean, after slipping into Savoie St Juste for coffee and rolls, had returned to supervise.

It was bitterly cold again and the sky was leaden. The earlier frost had brought down a lot of leaves and they lay now, brown and withered, on the frozen mud, the branches above stark against the iron sky.

Cold and bored, Nosjean had helped about the farm for some time and in the end had wandered off into the woods. They'd all been so busy searching the farmhouse and so much had happened, nobody had properly checked Bique à Poux's hideout. It had been his intention to do it long since, but the discovery of Vallois-Dot's body had thrown things out of joint a little and it seemed now was a good time to put things right.

Leaving his men busy round the farm buildings, he walked through the trees to where Bique à Poux's camp lay. It looked exactly the same as before – spartan and curiously lonely and damp-looking in the icy mist, now that it was unoccupied and the fire was dead. It seemed to be full of empty bottles and opened cans and there were tracks of mice and small woodland animals, as though, in the absence of its owner,

they'd come exploring for food. There was a saw in the lean-
to, he noticed, an axe, a butcher's cleaver, and a thin knife,
all sharp; and as he poked about, he noticed there were a
great number of feathers, some of them black and white like
the feathers of Matajcek's Marans. There were also a lot of
chicken bones – wing bones, leg bones and breast bones.

Nosjean smiled, deciding that at least he'd found the
identity of the chicken stealer who'd been bothering the
district. Then, opening the tent and turning over more rags,
he found himself staring at a parcel carefully wrapped in old
clothing. Unfastening it, he found a plastic sheet, and,
unfastening it further, found inside a deadly, long-bladed
knife of the sort issued to commandos during the war.
Alongside it was an old and heavy British Colt .45 revolver,
four of its chambers full of bullets.

He turned the two weapons over in his hands, holding
them carefully with a handkerchief. Unlike the rest of the
camp, which was as filthy as Bique à Poux had been, they
were carefully cleaned and lightly oiled, and as he worked
the chamber of the revolver, it moved easily.

Nosjean thought for a while, then went on exploring.
Almost immediately, he found three more bullets in a tin. But
they didn't fit the heavy Colt and he realised they were .38
calibre like his own gun. Putting them carefully in a small
plastic bag which he took from his pocket, he poked around
a little more, suddenly excited, and almost immediately
found a blue paper band printed '1000 Francs', and rubber
stamped 'Crédit Lyonnais, Firmin'. He stared at it, frowning,
then, moving things around more hurriedly, found a bundle
of old magazines and papers. Among them was an ancient
copy of *Le Bien Public* of 1976, containing a report of the
murder of one Jochen Peiper, a German ex-SS colonel who'd
been living in France and been found shot dead in his
burning bungalow. The local police had put it down to
suicide, but Nosjean – come to that, everybody else in the

force – had assumed when they'd heard of it that someone had taken the law into their own hands. Peiper had led the Kampfgruppe Peiper in the Ardennes breakthrough in the winter of 1944/5 and been tried at Dachau for the massacre of American prisoners. Sentenced to be hanged, because of irregularities in the trial instead he'd been imprisoned until 1957, and someone, either French or American, had appeared to have disagreed even with that verdict. The case had been closed without an arrest, chiefly, Nosjean suspected, because nobody was talking and the police weren't pushing too hard.

Nosjean remembered the case well, but it was surprising to find it here, carefully kept among Bique à Poux's papers. Then, turning the old papers and magazines over, he suddenly realised he was looking at pictures of another man over and over again – laughing in a car, walking, talking to German officers – and he realised that they had been cut from German military magazines, from *Le Bien Public,* and other daily newspapers. Their dates were all 1944, and this time the man in the pictures appeared to be known as Sturmbannführer Heinz Geistardt.

For a long time Nosjean stared at the papers, then at the cuttings about Peiper, wondering where the connection lay. He knew there *was* a connection and, feeling he'd found something important, he decided it demanded another visit to Bique à Poux. Wrapping up the weapons and tucking the papers away, he set off through the trees at a half-trot to Matajcek's farm.

What he found when he reached it startled him enough to put all thoughts of another visit to the hospital out of his head.

His men had turned up another body.

This time it was a woman and it was wrapped in a blanket and had been found behind the barn. Scraping away leaves and noticing a patch of earth which appeared, under the recent pounding rain, to have sunk below the rest of the land, the sergeant in charge had realised it was roughly the same shape and size as a grave and had instructed his men to dig. The body had been found only four feet below the surface. It was dressed in shabby clothes and was in an advanced state of decomposition.

Pel stood near the farmhouse door with Judge Polverari, Doctor Minet, Misset, Darcy, and Sergeant Massu, who was telling them what he knew about Matajcek's wife.

'Came from Gray, I believe,' he said. 'I don't know for sure, though, because Matajcek didn't encourage visitors, and when she came to Orgny shopping she always seemed ashamed of her shabbiness and kept to herself.'

'She seems to be aged around fifty,' Minet said. 'Would that fit?'

Massu's dark head nodded. 'Yes,' he said. 'She was about that.' In fact, there were no problems of identification. When the body was lifted out, it was found still to have a pinafore round its waist and, though the pinafore was black with the seepage of water and soil, it had not rotted and in the pocket was a woman's purse. It was an old-fashioned leather purse and it contained nothing but a few centimes and the identification papers of the owner – Yvette Matajcek.

'Matajcek's wife,' Massu said.

It wasn't even hard to decide how she'd been killed, because the back of her head was crushed, and it appeared she'd been hit by something hard and heavy.

'Like Matajcek,' Darcy pointed out.

'It was just a hunch.' The sergeant who'd dug up the body was obviously pleased with himself.

'No sign of anything else?' Polverari asked.

'No money, sir, if that's what you mean. This place's full of holes where you could stuff it, and you'd have to pull it down stone by stone to find them all. I reckon it was built two hundred years ago. There are gaps behind the beams and between the walls, and the birds have built nests in some of them, and the rats in others. You can't see into them and you can't get your hand in.'

It was while they were talking that Nosjean managed to tell Pel what he'd found at Bique à Poux's camp.

'I think we've found the chicken stealer, for a start, Patron,' he said. 'And we might have something else, too.'

He fetched the commando dagger and the revolver from his car and laid them on the kitchen table, together with the three rounds of .38 ammunition and the bank slip.

'Those cops at St Symphorien had their pistols taken,' he said. 'They were .38s, and the bank was Crédit Lyonnais at Firmin.'

Pel picked up the bank label and studied it carefully, staring at it as if he expected invisible writing to appear. Was Matajcek involved in the hold-up at Firmin? Was he part of the gang, and was that where the money that Bique à Poux had mentioned had come from, the unexpectedly large sum in his account. Had he been using his farm as a headquarters for them for some time or as a staging post for their escape? Had he been attacked because he'd wanted to back out of the affair or because they'd feared he might give them away?

'Ring Firmin,' he said to Nosjean. 'Check with the cashier of the bank. Find out if any of the robbers corresponded to Matajcek's description.'

'Right, Patron.'

'Then go and see Bique à Poux. He said he saw Matajcek with a lot of money. Ask him if he saw anything else. And find out where he got this slip and these rounds of ammunition. You might also ask him, while you're at it, what he was doing with a .45 Colt and a dagger honed sharp enough to shave himself. Perhaps he was the man who did all that throat-cutting he talked about.'

The bank wasn't very helpful. The cashier had seen the four men who'd held them up, but he'd been too scared to take in much. But he was certain that none of them was as old as Matajcek.

'They were young,' he said. 'In their twenties or thirties. This guy of yours must be much older.'

'Sixty-three to be exact,' Nosjean said.

'Not the age for a bank robber. And they didn't wear the sort of clothes you say *he* wore. They wore tight trousers, jeans probably, and windcheaters.'

'Colours?'

'Various. There was a blue one with those red and white stripes down the sleeves that everybody has these days. There was a red one, too, I noticed, with black lines down the sleeves. The others – ' the clerk frowned '– the others I can't remember. Dark, I think. Black or navy blue.'

Putting the telephone down, Nosjean stared at it for a while, then, acting on a hunch, he picked it up again and rang the criminal investigation department at St Etienne.

'These four chaps who robbed the bank and murdered those cops,' he said. 'Have you anybody lined up?'

'Yes, we have,' he was told.

'Any names?'

'Yes. Gaillard, Jean-Marie, and Calet, Henri. They're locals and they've disappeared. They have a record of this sort of thing further south. They've been working Marseilles and we think they might have picked up a few friends.'

'And the other two?'

'One's a Spaniard called Cossio, who was operating down Perpignan way and also seems to have disappeared. He's been seen around with Gaillard and Calet. The other we don't know much about – but we've got a name: Jesensky. He's believed to be a Russian or a Yugoslav or something.'

'Czech? Could he be a Czech?'

'Could be. Not much's known about him.'

Nosjean put the telephone down and sat thinking. It didn't seem to be just a coincidence that one of the gang of four men who'd robbed the bank at Firmin and then murdered two policemen as they escaped was possibly a Czech and that Matajcek was also a Czech and had worked on the wood-cutting at Bussy-la-Fontaine. He wondered if Matajcek had been the brains behind the gang.

He took his theory to Pel, who eyed him speculatively. 'You know,' he said. 'One day you might make a good detective.'

Nosjean smiled. 'Thanks, Patron,' he said.

Pel frowned. 'But don't let it go to your head,' he advised. 'It won't be just yet. Try Bique à Poux again.'

thirteen

The old man was pathetically pleased to see Nosjean.

'When are they going to let me out?' he asked.

'Soon.'

'I'll escape if they don't.'

'Why are you so keen?' Nosjean asked. 'Why not get better first?'

'I have to get home.'

'Why?' Nosjean asked. 'Because you're scared someone will root around your camp and find something they shouldn't.'

He knew at once from the old man's face that he'd touched a raw spot. Bique à Poux seemed to withdraw at once.

'No,' he said. 'I've nothing up there people can't see any time.'

'Not even a .45 revolver, a commando dagger, three rounds of .38 ammunition and a bank slip marked "1000 francs" and stamped "Crédit Lyonnais, Firmin"?'

The old man seemed to cower on his pillows, and Nosjean leaned closer.

'Where did you get the .38 ammunition?'

'I found it.'

'Where?'

'On Matajcek's land.'

'Where?'

'Just outside the farmyard. I think someone had dropped it.'

'And the bank slip? Did you find that at the farm?'

'No. Further in the forest. I picked it up. It was just lying there.'

'What would it be doing there?'

'I don't know.'

'What about the dagger and the revolver? Where did you get those?'

'I got them after the war. There were hundreds lying around. The British parachuted them into France by the plane load after the invasion. Everybody had one.'

'What were you going to do with them? You also had an axe and a butcher's cleaver. Both sharp. What were you using those for?'

'For firewood. Chopping firewood.'

'Then what was the dagger for?'

'Skinning rabbits.'

'I don't believe you. The blade's too thick, and you have a thinner knife with a shorter blade. Much better for skinning rabbits. Not so bad for cutting throats, too, come to think of it. *You* didn't do it, did you?'

'No! Never! I swear!' The old man's protest came as an agonised bleat.

Nosjean decided he was telling the truth. 'What about the revolver?' he asked. 'Had you a licence?'

'No.' The word was a whisper.

'What was it for?'

'I used it to shoot rabbits.'

Nosjean grinned. 'If you hit a rabbit with a thing that size, mon brave, 'there'd be nothing left of it.'

'There'd be enough for me.'

'Come on, old man,' Nosjean said more sharply. 'I don't believe you. Were you carrying either of them when you were at the calvary that night?'

'No! No!'

'And who's Heinz Geistardt?'

'I don't know.'

'Why do you keep his pictures then? And why keep the pictures of Jochen Peiper?'

'He was an SS man.'

'I know. Peiper was here in France, wasn't he? He was murdered. A year or two back. Was Geistardt here, too?'

'He may have been.'

'You know damn well whether he was or not. I can check easily enough.'

'Well, yes, he was.'

Nosjean's heart thumped. 'Did he have anything to do with you?'

'It was him who sent me to Poland to work under the Compulsory Labour scheme in 1943.'

'And you were going to shoot him?'

The old man seemed to dissolve. 'He sent me to Poland.'

'He's the reason you were waiting at the calvary the night of the murder, isn't he?'

The old man's head jerked forward in a nod.

'How did you know he was going to be there?'

'I heard him say so.'

'When?'

'Three nights before. I was in the woods by the road. He was in a car.

'What car?'

'I don't know. I couldn't see. There was no moon that night. He was talking to someone about the de Mougy silver and they arranged to meet. He said he knew where it was and the other man wanted to know.'

'Did he mention any names?'

'No. But I know he had a woman somewhere.'

'How do you know?'

'I saw him with her. One day when I was in Savoie St Juste buying paraffin.'

'You recognised him?'

'I could never forget him.'

'What was her name?'

'I don't know.'

'How old?'

'Fifty-ish. I heard he had a girl round here when he was here in the war.'

'Go on. What else do you know about her?'

'Nothing. Except that when he was here in the war, she was only a kid – eighteen or nineteen. That age. He liked them young, they said.'

'What was he doing back here in Burgundy this time?'

'Perhaps he was after the loot. They pretty well sacked the de Mougy home, didn't they? They cleared it of silver. They even took the old Baronne's jewels.'

'Where did it go?'

'They said it went to Germany. But I think it's buried in the woods up there.'

'Why?'

'I don't know. I just do. Willie told me.'

'Who's Willie?'

'I don't know his other name. He was a German. He was a bit simple. He was a waiter in the German mess at the château. He was killed by the Resistance in 1944, I heard. He told me before I was sent off to Poland. It was worth a fortune. They cleared the place out. Then the Gestapo heard about it. Probably they wanted it themselves. By that time they were beginning to quarrel among themselves because it was obvious they were going to lose the war and they were trying to get everything they could to take home.'

Armed with Nosjean's information, Pel went to the Palais de Justice to see Judge Polverari.

155

It was always a good idea to work with the Palais de Justice. Once, you could do as you pleased and nobody said anything, but new laws and new decrees had changed all that, and nowadays all too often there was bad feeling between the two departments.

Fortunately, Polverari was cheerful and broadminded and always helpful.

'Think this one's connected with the others?' he asked.

Pel shrugged. He knew nothing – yet. It seemed too big a coincidence, but there *were* such things as coincidences.

'We'd better have a talk,' Polverari said. 'Come and have lunch with me.'

He chose a place in the centre of the city, well known for its food. Just across the aisle four middle-aged businessmen, all fat, were going through the ritual of a four-hour lunch. It was clear from the look of them that they weren't going to rise from their seats until it was time to return to their offices for afternoon tea.

Pel sipped a vermouth because it was too early for brandy or whisky and Polverari ordered coq-au-vin. Unfortunately it was an off day and the meal wasn't as good as they'd expected. When it arrived Polverari examined it closely. 'This isn't chicken,' he said.

'Yes, Monsieur,' the maître d'hôtel insisted, fixing the judge with an intimidating eye. 'That's a wing.'

'Looks more like a cow's hind leg,' Polverari said briskly. 'Perhaps it was a flying cow. Change it.'

It was changed. Pel was deeply impressed, feeling he'd never have dared – not in that restaurant – to accuse them of negligence. He'd have eaten it, its size notwithstanding, despite it sticking in his throat, despite being a Frenchman and above all a Burgundian, whose compatriots had a reputation for seeing they got the best.

Judge Polverari was quite unmoved. He was small and so shrunken he looked as if he'd been laundered too often, but

156

his appetite was hearty and he was totally indifferent to what people thought of him.

'They should try harder,' he said loudly so that everybody in the restaurant could hear and Pel cowered as the maître d'hôtel fixed him with a bitter glance. 'It's no wonder the owners of these old restaurants where nobody eats lunch in less than three hours are having to bow to the times and convert them into snack bars.'

The discussion on the murders was brisk. Unlike Brisard's, Polverari's comments were the comments of a man full of confidence and experience. He didn't badger Pel to solve the case on the spot, and was sympathetic, helpful and full of ideas, most of which were sound. They drank far too much wine and enough black coffee to keep Pel awake for a year, then Judge Polverari insisted on double brandies – twice.

It was magnificent but it left Pel feeling dreadful, and as he returned to his office his thoughts on the murder were sluggish. Why dump the damn man at the calvary, anyway, he thought, when there were quarries handy in the area, and almost every farmer in the district had constructed a dam on his land for his cattle? For a special reason? And if there were a special reason, then it had to be connected with the calvary? And the calvary was connected with old hatreds, long enduring hatreds that ought to have died.

Something at the back of his mind stirred, something that had crossed his consciousness some time before. He'd forgotten it in his interest in Piot, Marie-Claire Jacquemin and the Baronne de Mougy, but now it came back, insidious and insistent, connected with Vallois-Dot and the dead man at the calvary. Somehow, this time, it made more sense.

It touched on something else, too, something uneasy and frightening that went a long way back.

Darcy was in the outer office, staring at his notebook. He had a list of everyone who'd been in the bar at Orgny the night of the murder of Vallois-Dot.

'Practically every male in the village,' he said. 'And quite a few females, too.'

Among the plethora of names Pel noticed those of Grévy and Heutelet. Piot had also called in for a drink for a few minutes, and even Massu and his constable, Weyl, had leaned against the bar and taken off their kepis to down a beer.

'Everybody,' Pel said bitterly, 'except the President of France.' He found it difficult to settle to work. His indigestion was turning into an ulcer, he felt sure, he had a thick head, and would doubtless feel worse the following morning. He pushed away the pile of reports on his desk, struggled to roll a cigarette, threw it into the waste paper basket unsmoked, and went to the door. Darcy looked up.

'You busy?' Pel asked.

'A bit, Patron. I'm going out to Savoie St Juste to see if they know anything about Madame Matajcek. She used to do her shopping there. They might know something.'

'You can drop me at Heutelet's place.'

It was raining again as they drove out of the car park and the sleet in it stuck to the windscreen. Pel huddled in his coat as they drove, muffled up to his nose, deep in thought.

'Penny for them, Patron?' Darcy offered.

'I was just thinking,' Pel said gloomily, 'that I've caught Brisard's cold.' He gestured at the road. 'Turn off to Bussy-la-Fontaine. I want to go there first.'

His mind was still bothered by something he couldn't put his finger on – something he'd seen but not absorbed, and he sensed that it was at the calvary that he'd find it, because it seemed to have been with him right from the beginning.

Leaving the car by the house, they walked to the calvary. The area was still taped off but there were no longer any police there.

Stopping in front of the calvary, Pel stood with his collar turned up, his nose in the scarlet muffler he was wearing, his hat down over his eyes. The day was grey, the sky leaden with more snow to come, and the silence was intense, so intense that a branch, cracking suddenly in the cold, made him turn quickly. Then he heard the harsh cawing of crows over the higher ground and the sound made him more than ever aware of the atmosphere of the place, and terribly conscious of having overlooked something. A detective had to try every possibility on the board, and he'd missed one.

Watched by Darcy, he took a step nearer the cross to stare at the plaque. 'Fusillés par les Nazis,' he read. '7 September, 1944.' Below it were the names in alphabetical order and from the bottom of them the name, Vallois-Dot, leapt out at him.

Patrice Vallois-Dot.

That was it!'

He'd noticed the names when he'd first arrived at the calvary to investigate the murder of the unknown man, but he'd not read them carefully enough for them to register in his mind. Then, when the postmaster had been found dead, his subconscious had been trying to pass on the connection to him, the fact that the same name was on the calvary where the first murder had occurred.

Frowning, he bent to study the plaque.

'*Dominique Louhalle, Légion d'Honneur,*' it said and lower down, after a slight gap, there were eight other names.

Jean-Marie Cirois
Armand Duval
Edouard Evangeliste
Pierre-Thomas Grandcamp
Antoine Hugo
Richard Poupon
Roland-Andre Sanz
Patrice Vallois-Dot

Standing in the glade of the forest, with the grey mistiness of the year's end about him, cold and cheerless and dark, Pel was chilled by the old bitterness. He'd been only a small boy at the time of the Occupation and could remember remarkably little beyond the presence of men in strange uniforms who spoke a foreign tongue. He'd been protected by childhood from the talk of killing and by the fact that in Vieilly, where he'd lived, there'd been very little show of resistance, anyway, chiefly because there had been few safe places for the Maquis to hide. What resistance had occurred in Burgundy – and because it was the last place the Germans had evacuated in their retreat beyond their own frontiers, it had never been strong until the last months of the Occupation – had occurred in the high lands and thick forests of the Côte d'Or.

It had been a time of edgy nerves hidden by stiff faces and blank expressions, a striving for defiance if only to keep some measure of pride. It hadn't been the running battle you read about in books of memoirs. Most of those engaged in it had been mere boys who'd fled to the woods to avoid being sent to Germany to work. They'd lived for months in camps in the trees, lacking everything but spirit, and their weapons had been rusty firearms from farmhouse walls, dynamite stolen from quarries, and a few old grenades too dangerous to handle.

In the south round Grenoble and in the Hautes Alpes it had been different. Until France had been totally occupied by the Germans you'd even been able to see British films down there, and it had always been easier to organise against the future. In the north little could be done until the Germans had been busy with the invasion.

He stood staring at the monument a little longer, then he walked back to the car.

'Turn up anything along the border?' he asked as Darcy started the car. 'Anybody think our man might have come from their area?'

'Nothing, Patron.'

Pel was thoughtful for a while. 'Isn't there a bureau in Germany,' he asked, 'run by the Jews for the investigation of Nazi war crimes?'

'I've heard of one.'

Pel frowned. 'Find out where it is, and ask them if they know anything about this Geistardt Nosjean turned up.' He paused. 'You might also try the German police. They're pretty helpful. Give them all our facts and tell them we think our man might *just* have been a German.'

'Might he, Patron?'

Pel nodded. 'He might,' he said. 'He just might.'

fourteen

Massu's van with its broken wing-lamp was standing outside the Heutelet farmhouse when they arrived. Inside, in front of a roaring fire, Heutelet was sitting with his feet up on a stool, holding a magazine. He seemed to have been dwelling on a series of photographs of scantily-clad girls. Massu, holding his notebook, overflowed the chair he was sitting in and, as they entered, he looked up and his black eyes flashed.

'Just trying to find something out about Madame Matajcek, sir,' he explained.

Heutelet seemed to consider the arrival of three policemen all at once a cause for celebration and he produced a bottle.

Pel sat back. His mind was busy. Nine dead people, he remembered. Eight men and one woman. Louhalle, Duval, Cirois, Evangeliste, Grandcamp, Vallois-Dot, Hugo, Poupon and Sanz.

He became aware of Heutelet staring at him and realised he'd been lost in his own thoughts.

He started back to the present. 'The Resistance,' he said. 'During the war. You were in it.'

Heutelet smiled. 'I ran it.'

Pel nodded. 'Yes,' he said. 'You ran it. So what do you know about the calvary at Bussy-la-Fontaine?'

Heutelet exchanged glances with Massu, then he shrugged. 'It was put up in 1947,' he said. 'They raised the funds locally. It was dedicated by the bishop. They were putting up a lot of those things in those days and the bishop was always at it.'

'The names on it. Nine of them. What happened to them?'

Heutelet shrugged. 'The Germans left them lying there. In a row. Like butchered pigs. The local people carried them down and put red, white and blue ribbons on the coffins. There were hundreds of mourners, and a tricolour, but a German officer tore it down and said they were only gangsters.'

'What about the relatives?'

Heutelet's eyes grew angry. 'What about them? They had their grief. They wept.'

'Where are they now?'

Heutelet shrugged again. 'Some of the women remarried and moved away. Some died. It's a long time ago.'

'Go on. Let's have details.'

Heutelet thought for a while. 'As far as I know there are only three left in this area: Madame Duval. She never remarried. She has grown-up children and grandchildren now. Vallois-Dot's wife died, but his son ran the post office at Orgny. He's the one who – '

'I know who he is,' Pel said. 'There can't be that many people called Vallois-Dot round here.'

Heutelet nodded his agreement. 'No. The other's Grandcamp. His wife died but he had a son and a daughter. The daughter married an American after the war and went to the States. The son runs a travel agency in Dijon. Near the station. The rest – ' Heutelet's shoulders lifted in another shrug.

For a while, Pel sat thinking. Three relatives of the nine dead Resistance fighters – Duval, Grandcamp and Vallois-Dot. And now Vallois-Dot was dead. That left two. In addition there was Grévy, who'd murdered a German in his escape from Germany, Piot, whose father had been killed by the Germans, and old Alois Eichthal – Bique à Poux – who, according to what he'd told Nosjean, had cut a throat or two to get back home.

He looked up at Heutelet. 'Ever heard of a man called Geistardt?' he asked. 'Heinz Geistardt?'

Heutelet frowned. 'I knew *a* Heinz Geistardt,' he agreed. 'But that was a long time ago.'

'Yes,' Pel said. 'It would be.'

'He was an SS man. He was involved in that butchery on the Vercors massif, I heard.'

'Describe him.'

Heutelet did. The description seemed to fit the body found at the calvary.

'Tell me more about him.'

'He was a cruel bastard.' Heutelet frowned. 'He seemed to enjoy cruelty. He was the one who shot those nine people at Bussy-la-Fontaine. There are a few plaques on the wall in Dijon he was responsible for, too. Students mostly. Kids. He was always our main target. But we never got him.'

'Suppose he happened to come back?' Pel asked. 'Would someone *try* to get him?'

Heutelet smiled. 'They got Jochen Peiper, didn't they?'

'Who did?'

Heutelet smiled again and Pel suspected that, if nothing else, he was a party to knowledge that the police didn't possess.

'I don't know who did it,' Heutelet said. 'But I bet it wasn't for racing debts or because he was after somebody's wife.' He frowned. 'The arrogance of the bastards beats me. They came here in the war and sent people to concentration camps or shoved them up against a wall. Now it's all been over a few years they think they've paid their debts and come back as tourists – even to live, because it's cheaper. Not the ordinary Germans – I've nothing against them. The Nazis. The bastards who were responsible for it all. The Americans and the British and the International courts might agree to it, but Frenchmen never will. Nor will the Dutch or the Norwegians or anybody else whose country was occupied. Nor will the Jews – and, despite the efforts of the Germans, there are still a few about.'

'If Geistardt came back,' Pel repeated, 'would *you* try to kill him?'

Heutelet answered frankly. 'Yes.'

'You yourself?'

'Yes.' The answer was blunt and unequivocal.

'Did he harm you?'

'They harmed everybody somehow. I'd shoot him with pleasure.'

'You didn't, did you?'

Heutelet smiled. 'Why? *Is* he back here?'

'He might have been.'

'The body at the calvary?'

'It could be.'

Heutelet shrugged. 'If it was him, then I only hope whoever did it made the bastard suffer a bit first.'

'It's thirty-four years since,' Pel pointed out.

'It's not too long,' Heutelet insisted. 'You can't understand unless you were there. My brother was shot. Down in Roches. His wife's spent thirty-four years without a husband, his children thirty-four years without a father. It's never too long. The Jews didn't think it too long to capture and kill Eichmann. The people who got Peiper didn't think it too long either. Neither would I.'

'Geistardt was probably tortured. Why?'

Heutelet smiled. 'Perhaps they were trying to get out of him what happened to the de Mougy silver. They went through the place you know. They took all the silver, even the old Baronne's jewels, everything they could carry. I bet the Baron wouldn't mind getting his hands on him.'

It was a thought.

'What happened to the silver?'

'They say it's buried in the woods up here somewhere.'
'Why?'
'Because the Germans were in the woods a lot just before they all bolted back to Germany.'
'Who were?'
'Geistardt for one. They came up in one of those Kubelwaggons they had – little cars like American jeeps. They had spades in the back. I heard later that senior SS officers were making enquiries about the looting of the de Mougy place. Perhaps they wanted it for themselves. But they never found it.'
'How do you know they came to the woods?'
'We were waiting for them. Not to get the swag. To get Geistardt. But we waited in the wrong place. He got away. And as far as I know the swag was never found.'
'So if he came back, he'd probably come back for that, would he?'
'Probably.' Heutelet shrugged. 'It's a long time, but you never know. The bastard probably thought like Peiper that all was forgiven and that he could come and spend his German marks here to take advantage of the difference in currency. The bastards are everywhere these days, aren't they?'

As Heutelet finished speaking, Darcy pulled out the copy of the map of Bussy-la-Fontaine he'd obtained from Danielle Delaporte.
'Ever seen one of these before?' he asked.
Heutelet's eyebrows shot up.
'Where did you get that?' he asked.
'It came from Piot's factory in Dôle. His secretary said it was in a book that came from Baron de Mougy's place.'
Heutelet smiled. 'Well, yes, it would be.'
'Know it?'
'Yes. It's one I put out.'

'You?' They stared at him, startled.

'Yes. We got up to all sorts of things.'

'What are the crosses?'

'Hiding places.'

'For loot?'

'No. For guns.'

Darcy began to smile. 'Piot thinks they're for loot,' he said.

Heutelet's handsome old face broke into a grin. 'He won't get much loot out of *that* map,' he said.

'*Did* you hide guns?'

'No. That's the point.'

They had left the maps where the Germans could find them, because they liked looking for caches of arms and were always certain there was one on every farm in the district.

'They were so certain they were hated, you understand,' Heutelet smiled. 'And the reckoning was coming.'

The Resistance had merely obliged them and kept their nerves on edge by allowing them to find the maps, which were left in briefcases on buses or pushed through letter boxes as if they'd been posted by an informer. It had never failed to work. There had been a map for every farm in the district, one for Matajcek's, one for Vaucheretard, one for Bussy-la-Fontaine.

'They never failed,' Heutelet said. 'They'd come storming up and set to work. We loved to see them sweat.'

'Didn't they react? With shooting?'

'They liked to pretend they were very legal and they could never pin them on anybody. It was a bit nerve-wracking at times if there'd been some trouble somewhere and they were in a bad temper. They pushed you around a bit. But it was always worth it.'

'What happened when they didn't find anything? Weren't they suspicious?'

Heutelet shrugged. 'We always had excuses. The crosses were where we'd set rabbit snares. "You've called in all our guns," we said, "and there's no food, so we have to use snares." "After all," we said, "we don't want to spring them ourselves and we mark them so that everybody in the family knows." '

'Didn't they ever suspect you were having them on?'

'Probably. But they didn't dare take chances. And they were such humourless bastards. Sometimes, we said it was where we'd found mushrooms – *trompettes de mort* or *chantrelles d'automne*. Or snails. Food was scarce under the Occupation and we were all at that game. We told them that it was usual, if you found a place, to mark it on a map for the following year. Because they didn't know what it was like to go hungry, they believed us. Sometimes we said it was because we'd seen partridges. We always had an excuse and they never found any guns. They must have dug up half of Burgundy. On D-Day there'd have been a lot more resistance to the invasion but for the fact that the Germans had a couple of divisions digging up the French countryside.' Heutelet grinned. 'They never seemed to catch on. Not even to where the bars hung the pictures of Hitler. They had to show them – Hitler and Pétain. It was the law, so they hung them on the lavatory door. When they had the round-ups in the streets in the hope of catching people with arms, all the women wrapped up everything they could think of and went out and let themselves be stopped. It kept the bastards busy while the others hid what they didn't want finding.'

Pel listened silently. Heutelet was smiling but when he'd finished, his smile died abruptly. 'It seems funny now,' he ended. 'It wasn't funny then. Sometimes they shot people.'

There was a long awkward silence that was full of half-forgotten horrors. Pel finished his drink.

'The shootings that took place at Bussy-la-Fontaine,' he said. 'Did you know any of them?'

Heutelet frowned. 'I knew them all.'

'Tell me about them.'

'They were ordinary people. They believed in France. Most people didn't know whether to lay low or be active and most people live all their lives at half-throttle anyway. There were a few, though, who felt something had to be done, if we were to hold up our heads after the war.'

'And you were one?'

'Yes. So were these others. Some of us got away with it. Some didn't. They were caught.'

'What about Vallois-Dot? What was he?'

'Civil Servant. Worked for the post office, like his son.'

Grandcamp had had a smithy, Duval had helped at the bar. Cirois and Hugo were labourers, Poupon a garde-champêtre from the other side of Orgny. Evangeliste had been a cowman and Sanz had had an old lorry which he used to carry wood. Since he delivered it to the Germans, they had even let him have petrol.

'What about the woman – Madame Louhalle?'

'She wasn't a "madame". She wasn't married.'

'She wasn't?' Pel was confused and looked to Massu for confirmation. 'I thought there was a child.'

Heutelet smiled. 'It's happened before, hasn't it? Call it one of war's tragedies. The father was called up in 1939, I heard, and killed at Sedan in 1940, just before it was born. She'd expected him to come on leave just before the Germans broke through, but, of course, he never did. For a long time she was heart-broken, then she got herself organised. She sent the child – it was a boy, I believe – to relatives in the south somewhere and became an active member of the Resistance. I didn't know her well, but the woman who kept the hotel where she worked is still alive. She'd tell you more about her. Name of Foing. Kept the Hostellerie des Trois Mousquetaires.'

'Where is she?'

'She has an antique shop on the road to Dijon just outside St Seine l'Abbaye. It's a bit of a tip, because she's ancient now. But she'd know about Louhalle. If she's still compos mentis, that is.'

'Massu can run me there,' Pel said.

Massu looked up, his dark face surprised. 'I thought Sergeant Darcy – '

'Sergeant Darcy has to go to Savoie St Juste.'

Massu gestured. 'Well, my van's due for servicing, sir. And I've arranged for them to fix the lamp.'

'When?'

'I was on my way.'

'You could leave it.'

Massu shifted in his seat. 'I made the arrangements, sir.'

'Arrangements can be altered.'

'Sir, I – '

Massu frowned, worried, but Darcy jumped in. 'It doesn't matter, Patron,' he said. 'I can leave Savoie St Juste until tomorrow. It might be interesting to learn something about this Louhalle woman, in fact.' He thought of Joséphine-Heloïse Aymé. The last time he'd telephoned, there'd been faint signs of a thaw. 'I might even find a little something to buy for a friend of mine.'

They dropped quickly down into Orgny, rounding the corners at speed, the tyres whining. The clouds made the day dark and the woods looked black beyond the trees.

Pel stared at them thoughtfully, wondering just what it must have been like to live in them through all the winters of the war, as some people had. He gave a little shudder, deciding that, with his frail health it was something he could never have done.

'Stop in Orgny,' he said. 'Let's go and see this Duval woman and Vallois-Dot's widow.'

The village was empty except for a few women moving in and out of the baker's and a group of men outside the bar. Madame Duval lived near the post office at the back of the Mairie. She was a thin bitter woman whose life had obviously not been easy. She was a withered little creature with a long nose, a tight, stitched mouth and work-worn hands.

'Of course I hated the Germans,' she said. 'They killed my husband. But it was his own fault, wasn't it? Patriotism? Pride? I got nothing out of those. The pension they gave me never kept me and I had to bring up three children. And now they've all left home and never come to see me.'

'Do you ever go up to put flowers on the shrine?' Darcy asked. She gave him a dark flickering glance. 'Why should I? I did for a bit on his grave in the churchyard. But not for long. I told him not to join the Resistance, anyway. The Germans were swarming all over the place. They hadn't a chance.'

The post office was being run by a new postmaster – a young man with a mandarin moustache and dark glasses that made him look like a mafioso. Madame Vallois-Dot was also busy behind the counter with the switchboard.

She greeted Pel, almost smiling. 'They've said I could stay on,' she said. 'I'll be looking after the telephones. They've decided it's too much for one person and they've made it official.' Her face changed. 'After all those years of my husband trying to do it on his own, too. He ought to have insisted before – before –' her voice trailed away, then she shrugged. 'He was never one to push himself, though.'

'Did he ever go up to Bussy-la-Fontaine?' Pel asked.

Her expression was startled. 'Why would he go up there?'

'To see Monsieur Piot, for instance. You said they were friends.' She shrugged. Only in the bar, she said. He had never gone to the shrine, to her knowledge, since she had known him, in spite of his father's name being on it. He might have done before their marriage, but she had always thought he'd forgotten the whole business.

Pel paused. 'What did he think of the Germans? Did he hate them?'

Her hand fluttered. 'Sometimes he said things. But nobody in France has much time for the Germans, anyway, do they? He was only a boy when his father was killed, though, so he was too young to worry much.'

fifteen

They found the antique shop on the hill as the road curved out of St Seine l'Abbaye. It lay against the rising ground, a whitewashed building with a long sloping roof that seemed on the point of falling in. Outside there were old cartwheels, rusting ploughshares, a sedan chair in a state of complete disrepair, prams and ancient barrows.

'It has everything,' Darcy said, 'but technicolour.'

As Pel pushed his way nervously inside the dark interior he found himself surrounded by Second Empire vases, ancient Norman cupboards and bedheads far too vast for any modern house, acres of statuettes, chairs, settees with the springs bursting out of them, heroic pictures of men and women, and statues of Napoleon by the thousand.

The old woman who appeared from the middle of the debris looked like a witch. She had on the remains of a dress which had once been good, but was now threadbare and faded. She peered through a pair of spectacles whose lenses had so many thumb marks on them they were virtually opaque and would have presented a problem to any fingerprint department.

'You don't look well,' she said at once to Pel.

Pel recoiled. It was always one of his horrors that he was about to drop dead, and to be told he didn't look well was enough to put him off his stroke immediately.

'I'll have to give you something for it,' she said. 'What are you after? A cheap bed because your son's got to get married

173

and can't afford to furnish his flat? A chair? A table? Perhaps you've bought a place in the country and need to furnish it cheaply?' She peered again at Pel. 'Yes, you need something,' she said. 'And I've got just the thing to put you right.'

Pel was clearly in retreat and Darcy joined in hurriedly. 'You used to keep the Hostellerie des Trois Mousquetaires near Orgny,' he said.

She peered at them over her spectacles – doubtless, Pel thought, because she couldn't see *through* them. 'Yes, I did,' she said. 'And I kept it well, too. I was younger in those days, of course. I gave it up after the war.'

'Do you remember a woman called Dominique Louhalle?' Pel asked.

The old woman stared at him, her eyebrows lifting, as if he'd conjured up a ghost.

'I've not heard that name for thirty years,' she said. 'Why do you want to know?'

'We have reason to suspect that the body found at Bussy-la-Fontaine is somehow connected with the names on the calvary,' he said. 'We're checking up on them.'

'I see.' She nodded. 'I know the calvary. I was there when they dedicated it. Because of Dominique.' She leaned towards Darcy. 'Are you sure your friend's quite well?'

'Tough as old boots,' Darcy said cheerfully. 'They'd pass him for jet fighters.'

'Oh!' The old woman took another look at Pel, obviously unconvinced.

'We've contacted everybody still alive who's related to the victims or remembers them,' Darcy went on. 'But Dominique Louhalle didn't have any relatives from round here.'

'No.' Madame Foing tore her eyes from Pel's face. 'She was from Marseilles way. And she looked it too. Not beautiful, but there was something about her vitality, *je ne sais quoi*. Dark and sturdy with jet-black eyes and thick dark hair. Strong back and a quick temper. There was nothing she was afraid of. Not even me. She wasn't always easy to handle.'

'Why not?' Pel asked.

'She answered back. But she was so good at her job I accepted it. She cooked for me. She was really only a child but she'd been well taught. She just had strong feelings about things and didn't hesitate to make them clear. She kept the kitchen staff in good order too.'

'How?'

'She hit them.'

'What with?'

'Her hands. They were big hands.'

'What about the war?'

The old woman gave them an arch look. 'She was rather a naughty girl,' she said.

'In what way?'

'She liked men. That girl's eyes turned a few heads in her time, believe me.' There was a wheezy cackle. 'But never as many as her behind. She got herself in the family way. I told her she could stay where she was until her man came home to marry her. Perhaps he never intended to, but anyway he never did.'

'So I heard,' Pel said. 'What happened then?'

'She was heartbroken for a while, then she took the child to relatives in the south somewhere, and came back to work for me. Because she wanted to hit back at the Germans. They hadn't occupied the southern half of the country at that time and she wanted her revenge. And that's what she got. She went to war.'

'She was brave, I understand.'

'She terrified me.'

'Did the child ever turn up again?'

'I never heard of it.'

'Do you have a photograph of her?'

'I had but – ' She turned and waved a hand vaguely at the heaps of old furniture behind her. They knew exactly what she meant. It was there somewhere, under the debris, but the chances of ever finding it were negligible.

'A pity,' Pel said. 'It might have helped. Is that all you know about her, Madame?'

'There's nothing else to tell.' The old woman shrugged. 'She came into my life like a rocket and went out of it the same way. Despite her faults, I admired her very much – especially later.' She peered again at Pel. 'I'm sure you're not well, you know. Let me give you a little dose for it.'

Pel looked at Darcy in alarm as she began to dig into a cupboard.

'It'll probably turn you into a frog,' Darcy whispered.

The old woman straightened up with a dirty glass and a bottle of wine. Into the glass she poured a little of the wine, then added a few drops of a yellowish liquid from a medicine bottle.

Trying not to breathe in, Pel swallowed the drink. The old woman smiled.

'It's also good for croup and worms,' she said. 'You haven't got those by any chance, have you?'

Pel spent the rest of the journey to the city in a state of extreme indignation and nausea, munching bismuth tablets as if he were a drug addict.

They called at a bar for a café-fine but they didn't serve coffee decaffeinated and they also seemed to be saving fuel, so that it was as cold as the North Pole.

'We'd better get on,' Pel decided hurriedly. 'We'll call on Grandcamp on the way.'

Maximilien Grandcamp's travel bureau was by the Porte Guillaume near the station. It was big and thriving, and Grandcamp, a plump red-faced man who looked as though he made a habit of living well, looked prosperous, confident and cheerful, in complete contrast to Madame Duval and Madame Vallois-Dot.

'I doubt if I've ever stopped to think about my father,' he admitted. 'I never really knew him and I just remember that suddenly I hadn't got one. One night he went out, I remember, and never came back. But I don't think it bothered me much after a while. I was too young for it to have much impact. I went to the funeral, of course, and saw all the red, white and blue ribbons. The Germans were there, I remember. That's about all.'

Pel was silent a moment. 'Georges Vallois-Dot,' he said. 'How well did you know him?'

Grandcamp thought for a moment then smiled. 'Not very well. He's dead now, isn't he? Am I being interrogated because of that?'

Pel didn't answer the question. 'How did *he* regard the Germans? Do you know?'

'Vallois-Dot? He hated them.'

'His wife said he never showed any signs of dislike, that he'd forgotten everything that happened.'

Grandcamp pulled a face. 'A man would in front of his wife, wouldn't he? But you have to remember I was at school with him. He hadn't forgotten them then.' He frowned. 'But he was a quiet chap – the sort who didn't say much. I think he detested his job – ' he smiled ' – I don't think he thought much of his wife, either, come to that, but I imagine he never let her know. He wasn't the type.'

'Do *you* have any feelings about the Germans?' Pel asked. 'After all, they shot your father.'

Grandcamp shrugged. He could see no point. After all, the Louhalle Group his father had been with had killed a lot of Germans, and in any case it was too many years since for him to feel much.

There was a long pause. A traffic snarl-up had formed round the stone archway outside and the hooting of horns drowned the ringing of telephones and the chattering of the girl assistants in the office. A policeman stalked past the window, hatred in his eyes behind the dark glasses he wore, picked his way through the jammed cars and started pointing, blowing his whistle and waving his baton. Intimidated, the traffic began to move at once.

Pel watched, quietly approving. He looked at Grandcamp. 'Ever heard of Heinz Geistardt?' he asked.

Grandcamp swung round in his chair. 'Should I have?'

'He was the man who had your father shot.'

Grandcamp frowned then shrugged again. 'I'd rather forget it,' be insisted stubbornly.

He'd always had it drilled into him by his mother, he said, that he should never forget but as he'd grown older there had been a different feeling and he'd preferred to let the matter drop.

Pel nodded agreement. 'Know anybody who *would* know Geistardt?' he asked.

Grandcamp shrugged. 'There was a woman, I heard. I don't know where she lived. But my mother was always talking about her. She said he had a woman somewhere.'

'A Frenchwoman?'

'Yes. Only a kid, I believe. Eighteen or nineteen. My mother detested the very thought of her. It always seemed to me, though, that she should have been pitied. I expect, with France as it was then, the Germans were the only people who had any money. Patriotism's a funny thing, isn't it? Some people can endure all sorts of horrors for it. To others it doesn't mean a thing.'

At the Hôtel de Police everybody had gone home but Nosjean, who was in a state of extreme agitation.

'The old man's bolted,' he said.

'What old man?' Pel asked.

'Bique à Poux.'

178

Pel was unmoved. 'Well, there's only one place he'll bolt to,' he said. 'His hideout. You'd better look there.'

In fact, they didn't have to look even that far because as they talked, the desk called to say the hospital had telephoned that Bique à Poux was back.

'Voluntarily?' Pel asked.

'Not likely. He's got a black eye and a cut lip.'

'Who brought him in?'

'Sergeant Massu, from Orgny. He found him leaving the city. He was on his way in to Traffic.'

'Go and see him, Nosjean,' Pel snapped. 'And while you're at it, inform Sergeant Massu that I'd like to see him. No sergeant from a sub-station's going to take it into his head to beat up one of my witnesses.'

As Nosjean vanished, Pel sat down at his desk and pulled a notebook forward.

'How do you feel, Chief?' Darcy asked.

'All right,' Pel said.

'How about your head? No little bumps growing at the front?'

'Little bumps?'

'Horns. The medicine.'

Pel glared, but to his surprise he realised that his incipient cold seemed not only to be better but that he also felt extraordinarily fit.

As Darcy vanished, he stared at his notes. Things were beginning to grow more clear to him. Whoever had shot the man at the calvary seemed to have shot him because he was a German and responsible for the deaths of the people whose names appeared on the shrine. So who was the murderer? Not Vallois-Dot, because he was dead. And Madame Duval was eaten with bitterness and didn't seem the type to go in for killing – whatever that meant – while Grandcamp claimed indifference. But Vallois-Dot had clearly been *involved*. Had he panicked, hoping that, because Geistardt was a wanted Nazi, the police would understand, and because of this had been killed in his turn to quieten him?

It was worth following up. Picking up the telephone, Pel called the police department at Grenoble and asked to speak to someone who could remember what had happened on the Vercors massif. It took some time because they were all too young, but in the end they unearthed a man working in Records who'd retired and was now employed as a clerk. He had it firmly in his mind.

'The people of Grenoble won't forget *that* for generations,' he said.

The Maquis had set themselves up in the hills. They had decided that since the invasion had started it was time to make a move. They had hung out flags and sung the *Marseillaise,* and for days they'd thought they could defy the Germans. But in the end the Germans had sent in gliders and armour, and then the SS and the Gestapo had gone to work. Men had been shot and tortured. One woman had been raped seventeen times with a doctor holding her pulse. Another, a Maquis officer, had been disembowelled and left to die with her intestines wound round her neck.

'It was as bad as Oradour,' the ex-policeman said. 'That was slaughter. This was deliberate torture.'

'Who was responsible?'

'Nobody ever knew. We thought a man called Geistardt was involved, but when he was brought to trial after the war, they couldn't make the charges stick. He got a seven-year sentence, cut to four for good behaviour. The crimes he'd been charged with weren't major ones and when more evidence turned up later he'd served his sentence and disappeared.'

Pel was thoughtful as he replaced the telephone. While he was staring at his blotter, Darcy appeared.

'The German Ministry of Justice in Bonn have been on the phone,' he said. 'The Commission they set up in Ludwigsberg for the investigation and prosecution of Nazi crimes still want Heinz Geistardt. Despite the fact that he got away with it at the war crimes trial, to them he's still a murderer.'

Pel was silent for a moment then he pushed the papers on his desk around. 'If it *was* Geistardt at the calvary,' he said, 'what was he doing on the Butte-Avelan? Was he hiding from the Jews? After all, they didn't hesitate to snatch up Eichmann and sentence him to death.'

'Perhaps he was just here on holiday,' Darcy suggested.

'Here?' Pel said. 'Where there are no resorts and there are men who'd give their right arms to meet him again?'

'Perhaps he didn't consider what he'd done serious,' Darcy suggested. 'At Nuremburg they admitted shootings without trial without turning a hair. It didn't even seem strange to them. They'd been ordered to do so. That was sufficient. They'd just obeyed orders.'

'But they didn't protest either,' Pel said. 'Do the Germans know where Geistardt is?'

'He was last heard of in Switzerland,' Darcy pointed out. 'But he's since disappeared. It's thought to Argentina.'

Pel frowned. 'Or to Burgundy,' he said.

sixteen

The thing was beginning to get on Pel's nerves. After considering it an affair that concerned Orgny and the countryside around, he had thought wrongly for a while that it was a mere domestic bitterness; now he realised that it *did* concern Orgny after all, but not in the way he'd first thought. It was deeper than that and he felt himself neck-deep in old hatreds and a bitterness that was suffocating. Having been only a boy during the war, he'd never realised the emotions it had engendered. Now it seemed to be welling up again, filling the valleys with fury.

It seemed to be time to go to the man who might really know the truth, and he rang the Baron de Mougy and arranged to meet him at the château at Ste Monique.

The Baron was much more formidable than his wife, a cold-eyed man almost two metres high, thin as a lathe with a frame that was still all muscle and sinew despite his age. Pel remembered he'd been a champion fencer, a dead shot and a ruthless and murderous Resistance leader, and decided he wouldn't like to be Piot if he discovered the liaison with his wife.

'Inspector Pel,' he said. 'Police Judiciaire.'

The Baron sniffed, as if he considered policemen a proletariat invention that couldn't possibly have any connection with himself.

'Wasn't there a Pel who was police commissaire for Avignon in the Twenties,' he said. 'I'm sure I've heard of him.'

He was so condescending Pel disliked him at once. 'There was a Pel who murdered his wife in Paris,' he said flatly. 'Felix-Albert Pel. Cut her up and burned the bits in the kitchen stove. It was at the time when Boulanger was trying to become President of the Republic. There were a lot of funny things happening in those days.'

De Mougy gave him a quick look but he didn't say anything and, with him effectively put in his place, Pel laid down the map of Bussy-la-Fontaine that Darcy had obtained from Dôle. 'Have you seen this before, Monsieur le Baron?' he asked.

The cold eyes glittered. 'Of course.' The words were clipped and sparse like the Baron. 'Heutelet telephoned me.'

Pel's eyebrows lifted. 'About this?' he said.

'No. About something else. He said he'd explained about that.'

'Yes,' Pel agreed. 'He did.'

'Then why ask me?'

'Merely as a check, Monsieur. What is it?'

The Baron frowned. 'It's a map we put out to confuse the Germans during the war.'

'Did it confuse them?'

'Often.'

'Were you in the château here when they were in residence?'

'Of course not.'

'Where were you?'

'In the woods.'

He wasn't exactly forthcoming, Pel thought, and he was having to dig out the facts with a trowel.

'Where, Monsieur?' he asked.

'At Illy.'

'What about the Germans here?'

The Baron's thin mouth moved. 'We shot a few,' he said.

'What about when they looted your château?'

'We shot a few more.'

Pel hesitated for a moment. 'Did you ever recover any of the loot?' he asked.

'Just one silver plate.'

'Where?'

'It was found in a ditch near Bussy-la-Fontaine – Piot's place.'

'Does Piot know?'

'I imagine so. Everybody else does. It was returned to my father.'

'Did you do anything about it?'

'We searched Bussy-la-Fontaine after the war. Monsieur Heurion was most helpful.'

'But you found nothing?'

'Not a thing.'

'No sign?'

'Not one.'

'Did you ever learn where it all went to?'

'No.'

'Had you no idea?'

'I heard later it was on Heutelet's land. Or on that lout Matajcek's.' The Baron's broad shoulders lifted.

'But you don't know for sure?'

'Of course not or I'd have claimed it.' Ask a silly question, Pel thought.

'Did you ever meet a German called Geistardt?' he asked.

The cold eyes flickered. 'Fortunately for him, no.'

'You knew who he was?'

'Yes. Sturmbannführer Heinz Geistardt. He was a murderer. It was my dearest wish that I might meet him.'

'What would you have done if you had?'

The Baron blinked. 'Shot him,' he said. He sounded as if Pel ought to have known.

Pel's thin dark face melted in a smile. 'That's what Heutelet telephoned about, isn't it?' he said.

The Baron frowned. 'Yes,' he snapped.

'Because he'd heard Geistardt had been seen.'

'Yes.'

'He never paid for his crimes, did he?'

The Baron shrugged. 'American-British soft-heartedness. They lean over backwards to explain away the acts of criminals.' He seemed to be warming up at last and his face had reddened. 'But for them we should have hanged the lot – guilty or not. But, of course, Britain and America were never occupied. The Dutch and the Norwegians would say the same as us.'

So had Heutelet, Pel thought.

'What do you know about Geistardt?' he asked.

The cold eyes were full of anger now. 'He was a murderer and a torturer of Frenchmen.'

'In addition to that.'

'Could there be more?'

'There might be. I need to find out. I would appreciate your help.'

The Baron considered. His nose wrinkled as if Pel were a bad smell. 'He was a characterless monster' he said. 'What can one say about a mere boy?'

'He was a *boy?*'

'Twenty-two or three. No more. I suspect he had influence with Himmler to be so important. He was the sort who tortures puppies or pulls the wings off flies. The school bully who enjoys seeing the smallest children weep.'

'What did he look like?'

'Fair-haired. Blue-eyed. Tall. Not sturdily built. But I imagine he wasn't a weakling.'

185

It all fitted the description of the corpse, Pel thought. He seemed to be getting somewhere at last.

'What else do you know about him?'

'He was a swindler.'

'Oh? In what way?'

'Every way you can think of. He made people hand in their papers then charged to get them back. He operated a protection racket round the bars. And round the farms. If you didn't pay, you found your animals commandeered. He extorted money from my father by saying that his paintings would go to Germany. They went anyway.'

'Anything else? Characteristics?'

The Baron's mouth curled in a sneer. 'What would you call these but characteristics?'

'I need more, Baron.'

'He was sadistic. He *enjoyed* torture, I think. He was also a womaniser. And always with *young* women. Girls almost. Seventeen, eighteen, nineteen. That age. I think he enjoyed their terror.'

'Would you know anybody he might have had occasion to visit?'

The Baron's mouth twisted in contempt. 'I can't imagine him being welcomed anywhere.'

'What about the women you mentioned?'

'They wouldn't dare. In any case, they all moved away after the Liberation. I've no doubt they decided it was safer. It wasn't entirely their fault, I realise, but not everybody knew that.'

Pel persisted. 'Wasn't there *one* courageous enough to stay and face people?'

De Mougy paused. 'There was a woman.'

'In Orgny?'

'You know one such?'

'I might,' Pel said.

The Baron shook his head. 'No. Not in Orgny. She lived in Savoie St Juste. She went away but she came back.'

That was what Bique à Poux had said. Pel leaned forward. His mind was on Madame Grévy. 'Do you know her name?'

The Baron sniffed. 'Who would forget the name of a woman who went with a man like Geistardt? Yes, I do. It was Charpentier. Denise Charpentier.'

Pel was surprised. This was a name they'd not heard so far. 'And she fraternised with Geistardt?'

'That's hardly the word to describe what she did.'

'You knew her?'

The Baron's hand moved in a gesture. He had never seen the woman with Geistardt. Savoie was some distance away, but all the stories indicated that she was Geistardt's woman. If he hadn't lived with her, he had always been at her house, a green-painted one at the end of the village. It was still green, in fact, because he'd seen it as he'd driven through.

Pel looked excited. 'Is *she* still there?' he asked.

'I think so.'

Pel's heart leapt. 'I think I'd better go and see her,' he said.

He was about to leave when the Baron stood up. 'If Geistardt *has* returned,' he said. 'I hope you catch him. If *you* don't, someone else will.'

'They probably have already,' Pel said. 'I think he was the man shot and tortured at the Bussy-la-Fontaine calvary.'

De Mougy's eyes glittered. 'I trust so,' he said. 'It would be poetic justice. He shot and tortured the Louhalle girl.'

'You knew *her*?' This seemed to be an unexpected bonus. The Baron nodded. 'Very well.'

'She was brave, I believe.'

'Superlatively so. She was quite indifferent to danger and the real leader in that area, whatever Heutelet claims. The men would never admit it, of course, but she was. I was the one who recommended her for the posthumous Légion d'Honneur.'

'Who received it for her?'

'I did. There were no relatives. It's in the Resistance Museum now.'

There seemed to be a desperate need to know this legendary fighter.

'Why was she so courageous?' Pel asked.

'Perhaps because she'd nothing to lose. She gave the Germans a lot of trouble at a time when nothing was organised round here and they took it out of her when they captured her. They did terrible things to her. Up there in the woods. Not to get information, you understand. Just because she'd been a nuisance to them.'

'How do you know this?'

The cold eyes flickered again. 'I was there when they were found. She was lying separate from the rest.' The thin face grimaced. 'I wouldn't like to say what they'd done to her. It was Geistardt who did it.'

'How do you know?'

'We had our sources of information. Unfortunately, they weren't firm enough when he was brought to trial and he got away with it. I was disgusted. He was a fastidious man and I think he made it worse for her because of what she was.'

'What she was?' Pel leaned forward. 'What *was* she?'

The Baron's eyebrows rose. 'Didn't you know? She was a tart.'

Pel's jaw dropped. This didn't seem to fit the picture of a heroine.

'A tart?'

The Baron smiled for the first time. 'Every man round Orgny – every man in the group – had her. I had her. I expect old Heutelet had her. He had every girl for miles around who was willing and I believe he still does.'

Pel found it hard to accept. 'She was a *prostitute*?'

'She took money for it.'

188

Pel was silent and the Baron went on. 'You look startled, Inspector. You needn't be. The heroes of the Resistance weren't all noble men and women. All too often they were the people who didn't fit well into society and therefore fitted well into the Resistance.'

'*You* were one, Baron.'

The Baron smiled. 'I was part of a privileged class. The wealthy never give a damn what people think and the poor can never afford to. It's the middle classes that play safe, both now and during the war. Some of the best of the Maquis were either the aristocracy, who were indifferent to conventions, or the gangsters and small-time city thugs, who'd lived by their wits all their lives. For them the Resistance was merely an extension of their peacetime behaviour. Because Dominique Louhalle was a tart was no reason why she shouldn't be brave. And, unlike the Charpentier woman and one or two others, she was never a *German* tart.'

seventeen

The Charpentier woman still lived in the green house at the end of the town of Savoie St Juste. She was a plump little creature who ran a laundry. According to the police sergeant Pel questioned first, she rarely spoke to people and apparently didn't wish to.

'Why should I?' she said when Pel visited her. 'That was a difficult time and it's best forgotten. We had a weight on our shoulders, a terror of the future, the constant worry about food, and the fear of being deported.'

Pel nodded. Even now he could recall how nobody had dared to do the things they wanted, nursing hatreds and fears, mistrusting people who seemed better off than they were themselves, despising the black marketeers yet, at the same time, having to accept that they were necessary. It had seemed as if the whole of France had lived in slow motion. It had been the darkest, emptiest, most anguished hour in the history of France.

'They shaved my head,' Denise Charpentier said. 'They cut off my hair and tattooed me.'

Pel looked up. 'A tattoo?' he asked, his interest caught at once. Would it match the one in the jar in Leguyader's laboratory?

'Can I see this tattoo?' he asked.

She gave him a bitter look. 'No, you can't,' she snapped. 'And there are two of them. Swastikas. One on each breast.'

190

The reply shook Pel and he went on uncertainly. 'You'd been –' he paused, and ended with a rush ' – friendly with the Germans?'

'With one of them.' The angry look deepened. Her husband had been murdered, she considered, by French politicians of the Third Republic who had sent him off to war half-trained and ill-equipped. He had been called up in September 1939, and by June 1940, he was dead. But she hadn't become friendly with the Germans because of that.

'Then why did they tattoo you, Madame?'

'That was when Hannes came.'

'Hannes?'

'That's what I called him. He said it was his name. We fell in love. He was good-looking and needed mothering.'

'Mothering?' It didn't sound like Geistardt. 'Please go on, Madame.'

She sighed and shrugged. 'He was a weak sort of man. Perhaps that's why I liked him. He wasn't like the other Germans. They were all arrogant and expected the girls to fall for them merely because they were conquerors. They never understood the hatred. It always puzzled them. *He* was different. He understood.'

This was a view of Geistardt Pel hadn't expected. But it took all sorts, and criminals, murderers and torturers often had some hidden depths.

She gave another sigh. 'He said it was because he'd fallen foul of the police in Koblenz when he was young.'

It was because of this that he'd grown bitter, she went on. All he'd done was steal a few vegetables when he'd been working in a warehouse between sessions at the Polytechnic. He'd been a student then and needed the money to live on. He'd considered the middlemen were making too much profit and, thinking he should have a little, too, had slipped an occasional crate to one side to be sold privately.

The old, old story, Pel thought. It was always somebody else's fault.

'Have you ever seen him since the war, Madame?'

She gave him a wary look. A few times, she admitted. The last time about a fortnight ago.

Pel began to feel that at last they were really getting somewhere. The false starts and the false trails they'd pursued seemed to have come to an end at last.

'Were you intimate with him, Madame?'

She gave him another sharp look. 'No,' she said. 'Only as a girl.'

Then, she'd just been married and enjoyed what happened between a man and a woman. When her husband had been killed, sometimes she had cried herself to sleep for want of a man. Pel made no comment and she went on angrily.

'It didn't last long. Then he left the village. He was posted to Ste Monique. To the Château de Mougy.'

It had pleased him, she went on, because he thought it gave him an opportunity for promotion. 'He was only here for a few months,' she ended, 'but it was enough for me to have my head shaved.'

Pel shifted uncomfortably in his chair. 'Do people here remember you?' he asked.

She shrugged. A few, she admitted. But she had let the house and gone to Paris to work. When the people she let it to had died, she came back. She had never asked for friendship, and she had never forgotten what had been done to her.

'I only came back,' she ended, 'because my son had qualified and left home.'

'There was a son?'

'Yes. He was a good boy. He's thirty-five now and in Argentina. I'm waiting for him to send for me.'

'Does he know his father was a German?'

She shrugged. 'I never told him. He thinks his father was killed in the invasion. He thinks he was one of de Gaulle's men.'

'Did his father know he had a son?'

'Not then. Later.'

'When later?'

'This year. He was driving to the south and he came through here. He saw me in the garden. I told him then.'

'Did he suggest marriage?'

'No. There was a woman in Germany and I didn't love him any more. Too many years had gone by.'

'Why did he come, Madame? To see you?'

She stared at her fingers then she gave a sigh. 'No. I didn't even have that pleasure. He was going to Orgny, that's all. He was doing some business. Some property or something.'

'Who with?'

'A Monsieur Piot, he said. He wanted to buy some land.'

'Bussy-la-Fontaine's forest land. Was he interested in forestry? Was he an expert at it?'

'No. He didn't seem to do anything special. He just said he thought it would be very profitable.'

Pel took out a copy of the map of Bussy-la-Fontaine Darcy had obtained from Dôle.

'Ever seen that before?' he asked.

She glanced at it. 'No. Should I have done?'

'It's a map of Bussy-la-Fontaine. It's marked, you'll notice, with crosses, and there are comments in German.'

She looked puzzled, and Pel went on briskly. 'I think – or shall we say your German friend thought – that it indicates the whereabouts of the de Mougy plate. You've heard of that, of course?'

'Yes.'

'I think your friend had one of these. Did he ever show it to you?'

'No.' She looked puzzled.

'Did he say he'd come and see you again?'

She hesitated then she nodded. 'Yes. In a day or two, he said. I was pleased. I was flattered that he wanted to. He gave me some money. Quite a lot because he didn't seem poor.' She hesitated. 'Perhaps it wasn't honest money. I don't know, but it pleased me that he wished to give it to me. I looked forward to seeing him again.'

'But he never came?'

'No.'

Pel studied his notebook. 'Was he involved in the theft at Baron de Mougy's place during the war?' he asked.

She shrugged. 'Perhaps. I don't know.'

'Did he mention it?'

'Yes.'

'*Could* he have done it?'

'Well, he wasn't entirely honest. I knew that.'

Pel shifted in his seat. 'Not entirely honest' were hardly the words for Geistardt. Geistardt was not only a swindler, he was a murderer, even a torturer. Perhaps she'd never realised just what he was because she'd been only just out of childhood at the time.

He paused. 'Did he have a bullet wound in his calf, Madame?' he asked.

She nodded. 'Yes. Right calf. Somebody waylaid the truck he was on in 1943 and he was wounded. It wasn't much.'

'And a tattoo?' Pel touched his right forearm. 'Here?'

'Yes. It was a regimental badge with his number. He tried to get rid of it with pumice stone. People used it to get their hands clean in those days and he always used to carry a piece in his pocket and work at it as we talked.'

Pel produced a photograph. 'Would that be how you remember it, Madame?'

She stared at it. 'Yes,' she said. 'That's how it looked. There was more of it then, of course.' She looked at Pel, with

194

agony in her eyes. 'He's the man they found in the forest, isn't he?'

Pel sighed. 'I'm afraid he is, Madame. Would you still have a photo?'

She fished in a drawer and produced a faded picture of a young German soldier in his shirt sleeves with his arm round a girl. The girl was slim and fair and bore no resemblance to Madame Charpentier, but the man could well have been the victim at the calvary.

'That is you, Madame?'

'Yes. And that's Hannes.'

'Heinz Geistardt?'

'No. Hannes Gestert?'

'Geistardt, Madame,' Pel said. 'Heinz Geistardt. Same man, I think. An officer in the SS.'

She stared. 'Then you can think again,' she said sharply. 'I wouldn't have been seen dead with one of *them*. Hannes was never in the SS. He wasn't even a Nazi. He despised them. He despised them all. From Hitler downwards. Because of the hatred they'd brought on Germany. He used to say it would take a dozen generations to break down what they'd built up. He'd never have joined the SS. He was in a sicherungsbataillon. He was an engineer and not even an officer.'

eighteen

Pel was shaken.

He'd been absolutely certain this time. Even the tattoo had seemed to suggest Geistardt. Many of the SS men had had skulls and crossbones tattooed on their arms, sometimes even their numbers, and it would make sense after the war that they'd want to get rid of them to hide what they'd been.

But the man murdered at the calvary was *not* Heinz Geistardt, though he'd been of the same nationality, build and colouring, and possessed roughly the same name, and the gossip the Baron had heard had been wrong. The woman at Savoie St Juste had been the mistress of a mere corporal.

On the way back to the city, Pel decided to see Piot.

He was driving a digger in the valley behind the house when Pel arrived and Pel had to walk down the winding muddy paths to find him.

'What are you digging?' he asked.

Piot smiled. 'A dam.'

'Why? You have a spring to supply water. The place's even called Bussy-la-Fontaine.'

Piot smiled again. 'I'm going to stock it with perch and a few trout. There's nothing like a fresh trout, Inspector.'

'You already have a dam on your land.'

Piot shrugged. 'That's to supply the eastern end with water. This one's to supply the western end.'

'And the digging to the north? What's that?'

Piot didn't hesitate. 'Road,' he said briskly. 'To make it easier to get the logs away when the contractors come.'

There was a pause as Piot climbed from the digger. Alongside the car he offered Pel a cigarette. Gloomily, Pel took it and lit it.

'I've found out who the young lady is who was staying here,' he said. 'Madame Grévy was right. It wasn't your cousin, was it? It was the Baronne de Mougy.'

For a second – just for a second – Piot's face became hard.

'How do you get on with her husband?'

'How does any man get on with the man he's cuckolded?' Piot's smile came back. 'Warily, Inspector. I take care.'

Pel drew at his cigarette, sadly studying the smoke as he blew it out. 'Do business with him?' he asked.

'Yes. I have shops in Paris. I buy frozen food from him.'

'Have you ever discussed with him the looting of his château during the war?'

Piot's lips tightened and Pel was aware of a sudden withdrawal. Then he smiled and shrugged. 'I told your sergeant,' he said. 'It would be nice to find it. If only to return it to the Baronne.'

Pel paused, then switched the direction of his questions. 'You know a man called Gestert?'

Piot's eyes became veiled. 'Should I?'

'You're doing a deal with him. He's interested in buying some of your land.'

'Oh, *him!*' Piot's gesture was unconvincing. 'Yes, I know him. He fancied he could make more out of my land than I could. He'd been here with the German engineers during the war and he liked the look of it.'

'But you didn't accept his offer?'

Piot shrugged. 'I don't need his money. But I'm a businessman, Inspector, and if someone wants my property I like to know why. When I find out, I ask myself "Can I do what he wants to do with it, only better?" Usually I can. So I don't sell. That's what I decided in this case.'

'Because of the de Mougy plate?'

Piot shrugged.

'And that was the reason for your interest in the Baronne?'

'Of course not.'

'Did she ever tell you of the value of the plate?'

Piot smiled. 'It's surprising what you talk about in bed.'

Pel put on his police face.

'Your father was shot by SS Sturmbannführer Heinz Geistardt, wasn't he?'

There was a long pause before Piot answered. 'Yes,' he said at last. 'He was.'

'At Grenoble?'

'No.' Piot frowned. 'Near here. The other side of Arzy, to be exact. My father was one of those who escaped from the Vercors plateau. There weren't many. He came back to his home. That's where Geistardt found him.'

'How did Geistardt know he was there?'

'I expect someone told him?'

'Who?'

'Rumour has it that it was Matajcek. But I don't know. There've been a lot of funny stories about him. He never joined the Resistance, for instance, though you might have thought that, being a Czech, he'd be one of the first to do so. In fact, I believe there was a lot of suspicion about him being a German spy. It was probably just gossip, but he was never trusted.'

It had been a bad morning. The German police had come up with a few more answers, but none of them the right one. They knew Hannes Gestert all right. He had a record as long as your arm and they weren't sorry that he was unlikely to bother them any more. He'd been in and out of jail ever since youth, had spent several years in Argentina, working for a

German firm and getting himself mixed up with a lot of shady characters, and had eventually had to head back to Europe.

'Then he disappeared,' they pointed out.

'Yes,' Pel said. 'We've found him.'

In his frustrated disappointment, Pel took it out on Nosjean. 'Where's Massu?' he demanded angrily. 'Why hasn't he reported to me yet?'

'I told him, Patron,' Nosjean bleated. 'I told him you wanted him.'

'Get him!' Pel snapped. 'I want him in front of my desk. You're falling down on the job again.'

Nosjean went out, bewildered, and telephoned Massu. 'You'd better come in,' he said. 'Fast. Or it'll be worse for you.'

As he put down the telephone, Krauss handed him a message that had come from the hospital. It seemed their chief witness was dying.

Grabbing his coat, Nosjean hurried off at once, feeling he was running short of time because he was certain he hadn't yet found out everything Bique à Poux had to tell him.

When he arrived Catherine Deneuve's sister warned him he'd only got half an hour. 'After that,' she said, 'anything could happen.'

He stared into the ward. 'What was it?' he asked.

'Another heart attack. We were watching him carefully but he got out, as you know.'

'Would that have an effect?'

'If he tried to hurry. And I expect he did.'

'He got a black eye. Somebody hit him. Would *that* have any effect?'

She gave him a sad look. 'Bound to have,' she said. 'He's in a bad way, so go easy. I'm not having him badgered.'

The transformation in Bique à Poux was quite considerable. His face seemed to have fallen in and his eyes, large and blue-grey, were surrounded by enormous hollows that showed the formation of the skull. Even his nose seemed to have sunk back on its bony support.

'Was it what Sergeant Massu did to you?' Nosjean asked.

The old man shook his head. 'No. It's this place. I told you. They expect you to behave like everybody else. Breathe in. Breathe out. Drink your coffee. Eat your roll. Finish your soup. Go and empty your bladder. I can't live like that. Why don't they let me out?'

'They will when you're better,' Nosjean said.

The old man was under heavy sedation and was sleepy. 'It was me pinched those chickens,' he said suddenly.

'Yes,' Nosjean said. 'I know.'

The old man's eyes opened. 'You knew?'

'Your place was full of feathers and chicken bones. It didn't take much working out.'

Bique à Poux smiled tiredly. 'I had a good run for my money. I only went in for that when I discovered I got pains in my chest when I was after rabbits. It was easier, and there were always plenty. I saw some funny things.' His eyes opened again. 'Matajcek killed her, you know,' he said.

'His wife?'

'Yes. She was kind to me. Used to give me bread and sometimes soup. But Matajcek was a mean bastard. He was always quarrelling with her. He beat her up more than once because of me.'

'Why did he kill her?'

'Because she objected.'

'To what?'

'He got mixed up with a gang from Marseilles way. She didn't like them. Neither did I. They were a mean-looking bunch. All young and hard. They quarrelled, and she tried to hit him with the poker, but he took it off her and hit *her* with it instead.'

'How do you know?'

200

'I saw it happen. I waited my time.'

'You waited your time to do what?'

'To get him. I got him in the end with a spade.'

'It was you who hit him?'

The old man shrugged. 'It took a long time, but if I hadn't the others probably would have.'

'What others?'

'Those chaps from Marseilles. They weren't going to go on hiding in that barn for ever.'

'Which barn?'

But Bique à Poux was asleep.

When Nosjean went to report to Pel he was in his office, frowning at his desk and the scrawls in his notebook again. The Germans had been on the telephone once more. They'd been to see Gestert's widow in Koblenz. It seemed the Gesterts had spent a holiday the year before in the south of France and to get there had crossed the frontier at Breisach and headed through Vesoul for the autoroute south.

At St Sabrin, Gestert had stopped and stared round him, and had then diverted unexpectedly from their route via Savoie St Juste. He had marked the place on the map, which his wife still possessed, and when they'd returned to Germany he'd spent the whole day searching the attic for old papers he possessed, digging them out of an old kitbag in which he'd kept souvenirs from the war.

'And then?' Pel asked.

'And then, apparently,' the German policeman said, 'he announced he had business to do and he expected it to be good.'

His widow had noticed that he had a map of some sort and he'd left, saying he was going to Belfort. When she'd asked why, he'd announced that, with the German mark as strong as it was, it was a good time to invest in land in France. She'd never seen him again.

Pel sighed, then he became aware of Nosjean standing in front of his desk and he looked up, scowling.

'Where's Massu?' he said.

'Hasn't he been in, Patron?'

Nosjean looked puzzled and Pel glared. 'I don't suppose you told him,' he snapped.

'I did, Chief. He said he'd come.'

'Well, he hasn't,' Pel growled. 'Ring him again. I want him.'

'Yes, Patron,' Nosjean said. He explained what Bique à Poux had told him. 'Hadn't I better investigate a bit further?'

'Yes,' Pel gestured. 'Get out there. But first ring Massu and go along to Records and bring me his file.'

The file was a thick one. Nosjean laid it on Pel's desk and bolted. With a bit of luck he was hoping to have the night off and he wasn't taking any chances of jeopardising it.

As the door shut behind him, Pel pulled the file towards him and glanced at the title. 'Massu, David, Brigadier.' Turning at once to the end, he saw there were numerous commendations and good conduct marks and a recommendation for promotion on passing the necessary examinations. There were also several reprimands for using his fists.

It didn't tell him much, and he turned to Massu's career.

'Military service, 1960 – 62. *Provost* department, Metz, Limoges, Marseilles, Dijon, with a short spell in Algeria.

Where he'd doubtless learned to hit his prisoners, Pel decided.

He turned the sheet. 'Joined police October, 1963. Sous-brigadier 1969. Brigadier 1975.' There wasn't much there either.

He turned to the sheet covering Massu's background.

'Born Sept 17, 1940. Inmate of Bernard Massu Orphanage, Fontaine-les-Dijon.'

Pel's eyebrows shot up. Bernard Massu Orphanage! An orphan! So Massu wasn't his real name but one given him by the nuns!

He turned a page slowly, almost as if he half-expected something to jump out at him.

It did.

He was still staring at it when the telephone went. As he picked it up, the sergeant's voice came from the front office.

'Sergeant Massu from Orgny to see you, sir.'

Pel was still peering at the file as he held the instrument to his ear.

'Massu?'

'He said you ordered him to report to you.'

Pel came to life. 'Yes, that's right. Send him up.'

He put down the telephone and closed Massu's file slowly. Then, without thinking, he fished in his drawer and, taking out a packet of Gauloises, lit one and sat in silence, deep in thought. Though he was staring at the smoke rising in front of him, he wasn't seeing it.

When Massu arrived in his office, Pel had placed the file in his drawer. As the sergeant stopped in front of his desk, Pel looked up at him and went into the attack at once.

'Alois Eichthal,' he said sharply. 'Also known as Bique à Poux: Don't you like him?'

Massu scowled. 'Not much.'

'Why not? Because he's an Alsatian?'

Massu was silent for a moment before he answered. 'I didn't know he was an Alsatian.'

'What else would he be with a name like Alois Eichthal? He could only have been a German.'

Massu stared sullenly in front of him, his face dark. 'The man at the calvary was a German,' Pel went on. 'We've finally found out who he is. Have you heard?'

Massu's big shoulders moved. 'Yes. Heinz Geistardt.'

'No.' Pel paused. 'This chap *wasn't* Geistardt.'

Massu's heavy jaw dropped. There was a startled look on his face. 'He wasn't?'

'No. His name was Gestert. Hannes Gestert. It's a reasonable mistake for anyone to make, I suppose. Why did you hit Bique à Poux?'

'He was escaping.'

'It's not the job of the police to be judge, jury and executioner,' Pel snapped. 'I've been talking to the Chief, Massu. There seem to be quite a few instances in your career of people being beaten up because they were trying to escape. The Spanish call it *ley des fugas*. Law of flight. It entitles the police to shoot a man if he tries to run. The Germans used to do it, too. In France we don't.'

Massu's big shoulders moved again. 'I lost my temper.'

'Your temper's well known,' Pel said. 'You'd better get out there and write me out a full report.'

'Is it going to the Chief?' Massu looked worried.

'Never mind who it's going to. Go and do it. And don't come back in five minutes with it scrawled on half a sheet of paper. I want a full report properly written. Exact times. Descriptions. Everything. Take a long time over it. Take all day.'

As Massu vanished, growling, Pel sat staring at the door. After a while, he lit a Gauloise and for a long time sat puffing at it. Then he sat bolt upright and pulled the telephone towards him.

'Pel here,' he said as Leguyader answered. 'There's a little job I want you to do.'

nineteen

It was Heutelet who explained to Nosjean what Bique à Poux was getting at. 'Matajcek had a barn in the woods,' he said. 'It was built years ago. Long before the war. During the war, we hid our guns there. Matajcek used to hide stolen cattle. I think he had more than one from me in his day.'

'Where is it?'

Heutelet produced a map and jabbed a finger at it. 'There,' he said. 'It's falling down now. The roof's collapsed.'

Nosjean stared at the map. 'Can I get at it from here?' he asked. 'It's quicker this way than from the road,' Heutelet smiled. 'You can't drive up to it, but if you cross our land and go through the fence, you can drop into the valley. Then you just cross the stream and climb up the other side and there it is.'

Nosjean left his car at the Heutelets' and set off walking. The deep grass of the fields was wet with the recent rains, and his trousers were soon soaked and he could feel the water squelching in his shoes. After climbing through the fence, he descended into the valley, most of the way on his back, because the rain and the snow had made the banks muddy and his feet shot from under him as he began to climb down, so that he slithered all the way to the bottom, crashing and smashing through the wet undergrowth.

At the bottom he picked himself up, soaked, muddy and angry. The bank out of the dip was even more difficult. It was so steep and so muddy after the rain it was almost impossible, and he had to follow the valley for some way until he found a winding path upwards. It hadn't been used for years, but it was clear of big trees as if it had been made by farmers and labourers heading home across the fields.

After a while, through the trees to his left, he saw a rough stone wall in the shape of a gable, and a few beams that had once formed a roof. Deciding he'd see nothing from the back, he circled the ruin to approach it from the front. As he began to move forward again, he saw what looked like an area of heavily-matted undergrowth, but it dawned on him abruptly that the leaves were all dead and that it was, in fact, a hiding place of cut branches concealing a car.

Moving round it, he was creeping slowly nearer to the barn when he saw a splash of red through the trees. Dropping flat on his face he stared through the undergrowth. The red came from a windcheater with black lines down the sleeve and it was worn by a young man with long hair and a drooping moustache who was relieving himself into the bushes. As he did so, he spoke over his shoulder to someone and Nosjean saw another youngster appear through the door of the barn. This man also wore a windcheater, a blue one this time with red and white lines down the sleeve.

Two, Nosjean thought, and even as he did so a third man appeared and they stood in a group, talking.

Whoever they were, whatever they were up to, Nosjean suspected it was no good. Men didn't hide in derelict barns in the middle of woods in winter for no reason at all.

As his thoughts ran on, he heard a voice inside the barn and one of the three men turned and waved.

Four, he thought. Four!

For a long time, he remained where he was, watching, wet, cold and muddy but warmed by his discovery. After two hours he came to the conclusion there were no more than the four men he'd seen, and it seemed to be time to report to Pel.

Returning the way he'd come, he picked up his car at the Heutelet farm, taciturn as they questioned him, and drove to the city as if the hounds of hell were after him.

'Four?' Pel said. 'Describe them.'

Nosjean did so to the best of his ability.

'Four,' Pel mused. 'All young. All tough-looking. All wearing clothes that fit the description you got from the bank clerk. Get me the list from the sergeant in the charge office, Nosjean. Darcy, get hold of Lagé. He's been doing nothing at the hospital for days and we'll need him. *And* Krauss and Misset.'

When Nosjean returned, Pel was on the telephone to the Chief. 'It's obviously the same lot,' he was saying. 'They've been using the place – with Matajcek's knowledge, I imagine – until the uproar dies down. They've probably used it before, judging by the amount in his bank account. I'll want a squad of uniformed men. I want to surround the place. Yes, I can get the men from Savoie St Juste. And I'll take Sergeant Massu and his man.'

There was a pause and Nosjean distinctly heard the Chief say, 'I thought you didn't like Massu. You put in a note about him a couple of days ago.'

Pel's eyes flickered towards Nosjean and he gestured to the telephone. 'He's a good policeman,' he said. 'I don't like his methods and I don't like his temper, but he's got a good record for keeping his head in a crisis.'

While they were assembling their men, the telephone went. Nosjean answered it. It was Catherine Deneuve's sister to say Bique à Poux was dead. Nosjean put the telephone down, his face tragic.

'The old man's died,' he said.

Pel put a hand on his shoulder. 'At least he's clean and comfortable,' he said.

207

Nosjean frowned. 'I think he'd rather have been dirty and uncomfortable and alive,' he said.

Pel gave him a little shove. 'He had a good life, mon brave, and he's done us a good turn. Make it worth his while. There's a job to do.'

It only took a couple of hours to gather the men at Orgny. Massu was there, with his constable, looking faintly sheepish in front of Pel, and four men had come from Savoie St Juste. There were also a dozen from Dijon, together with Pel's squad, and a car with a man to handle the radio contact with headquarters.

Pel made his wishes clear. 'We surround the place,' he explained. 'Keep your ears to your radios because I don't want any move made until I give the word. Nosjean will lead one group from the Heutelet place, Sergeant Misset will approach from the direction of Bussy-la-Fontaine, and Sergeant Krauss from the opposite side. I'll lead the approach from the main road and Matajcek's farm. Understood?'

Heads were nodded and there was a lot of hitching at belts and straightening of képis.

'Report when you're in position,' Pel continued. 'I'll then give the word to go. But don't hurry. Don't go crashing about in the undergrowth like wild elephants. The idea's to catch them, not frighten them away. When I give the word, you can make all the noise you want. If they start shooting – and they probably will, because with two dead men behind them they've nothing to lose with another one – shoot back. You all got your guns?'

They nodded. 'I shall want you to account for every round you fire afterwards,' Pel said, and they looked at each other, puzzled, wondering what he was getting at.

'There may be more than we think,' he said. 'We'll need something in reserve. Off you go.'

There were six car-loads of men and they separated and headed in their various directions. Driving up to the main highway, Darcy turned left.

'Matajcek's place, Patron?' he asked.

'Yes. As fast as you can.'

Darcy glanced at him. 'You've got a look in your eye, Patron,' he commented. 'Is something in the wind?'

'More than you think,' Pel said.

'You think this lot's involved with Gestert and Vallois-Dot?'

'Not directly,' Pel said. 'But it'll sort itself out.'

'Here?' Darcy's eyebrows lifted. 'Arresting four bank robbers who murdered two cops in St Symphorien?'

'I think so.'

Darcy gave him another curious look but he knew Pel and decided he was best left alone in this mood. It would all come out in the wash.

They pulled up in the muddy lane outside Matajcek's farmhouse, where they left the cars, then, with Darcy leading, Lagé operating the walkie-talkie and Pel close behind, they moved quietly up the lane into the wood. Eventually, the lane became no more than a pathway and they started to push through the trees.

After a while, Darcy held up his hand, and they stopped, crouching down.

'I see red, Patron,' he whispered. 'It's a kid in a red windcheater.'

'Nosjean reports himself in position, Chief,' Lagé said quietly. 'Right.' Pel gestured. 'See if we can get a bit nearer. Spread out. Darcy, stay close to me. Lagé, you stay alongside, too.'

They moved a little nearer and halted again.

'Misset's ready, Patron.'

'Only wants Krauss,' Darcy said.

'He's bound to be last,' Pel observed. 'He's a dim flame, if ever there was one.'

A few minutes later Krauss reported in.

'Tell them to spread their men out and report back.'

After a while, the other groups reported themselves ready. Pel nodded. 'Tell them we're going in, Lagé,' he said. 'Come on, Darcy, let's go!'

They moved forward at a half-run, the undergrowth crashing before them. Almost at once the man in the red windcheater appeared by the barn. He called something to someone inside and a moment later a man in a blue windcheater appeared also. He carried a sawn-off shot gun which he fired in their direction. They heard the pellets striking the leaves and the boles of trees.

'Fat lot of good that'll do,' Darcy commented. 'At this range. Standing by the bole of a tree, he rested his right arm against it, steadying it with his left. The crash of the shot echoed through the wood and Pel saw the man in the red windcheater go head over heels.

Two more men had appeared now and there was shooting from Nosjean's party on the other side of the barn. One of the men ran to the back of the building but there was a fusillade of shots and he staggered back against the wall and slid down to a sitting position.

Misset's men and Krauss' men could now be seen on either flank, then Nosjean, leading his men forward as if he were storming the Malakov at Sebastopol. As they went forward, a thin shaft of sunlight lanced down unexpectedly, falling directly on the barn so that the men were illuminated as if by a spotlight.

'The sun of Austerlitz,' Pel said.

The firing was continuous now, and the man in the blue wind-cheater fell. For a while, they waited for the fourth man to appear, but there was no sign of him and they moved forward warily.

The man in the red windcheater was dead, shot through the heart by Darcy's first bullet. The other two were both wounded, but neither of them so seriously he wouldn't be able to stand trial for murder. Inside the barn were suitcases filled with money – five, Pel noticed, one doubtless for Matajcek – and two .38 pistols, one at the feet of a fourth man who was standing with his back to the wall, his hands as high in the air as he could get them.

Darcy whipped him round so that he was facing the wall, resting on his hands, his feet well back and wide apart. His gun in his fist, Darcy ran his hands over him.

'No weapons, Chief!'

'Manacle him.'

As the man was handcuffed, Darcy began to stuff his pistol away.

Pel stopped him. 'Let's have a look at that,' he said.

Darcy looked puzzled. 'Three shots, Patron,' he said. 'That's all I fired.'

'Let me see.'

'What *is* this, chief?'

'Don't argue!'

Darcy looked indignant. 'It's not usual, is it?'

'It is this time.'

Frowning, Darcy handed over the revolver. Pel broke it open, examined the contents, and handed it back. Darcy had begun to stuff it away again when Pel laid a hand on it.

'Keep it in your fist,' he said.

'Why?'

'You might need it.'

'We've got them all, Patron.'

'Holy Mother of God,' Pel snapped. 'Can't you do as you're told for once?'

Darcy stared at him, startled, but he kept the gun in his hand.

'Misset?'

Misset glanced at Darcy, equally puzzled, but he handed over his gun. Pel went through the same rigmarole.

'Krauss.'

'Patron, I didn't fire.'

'Don't argue.'

Krauss handed over the weapon. Pel broke it open, examined it and handed it back.

'Nosjean.'

'Look, Patron,' Darcy began, 'if we have to go through this performance every time we arrest somebody – '

'Massu.'

Massu scowled. 'I only fired one shot.'

Pel made no comment but stood with his hand out. With a shrug, Massu handed over the pistol. Pel broke it open but this time, instead of merely glancing at the rounds in the chamber, he tapped them out into his hand, studying them carefully. Then, slipping them into his pocket, he tossed the weapon to Darcy.

'See that Ballistics get a look at that,' he said. 'I think you'll find it's the gun that killed Vallois-Dot and our friend at the calvary.'

Darcy's jaw dropped. Massu was standing with his feet wide apart, his dark ugly face growing red. Then, suddenly he made a dive between Darcy and Pel and started crashing through the trees.

'Get him, Darcy!'

'Shoot him, Patron?'

'In the leg. If you don't hurry, he'll be too far away.'

Darcy crouched and fired. The first shot missed, but the second brought Massu down and, as they ran towards him, he lay groaning and clutching his thigh.

Pel stared down at him. 'I told you, Massu,' he said coldly. 'It's not the job of the police to be judge, jury and executioner. Especially when you get the wrong man. The man you and Vallois-Dot executed in the Plaine looked like

Geistardt. He even had a similar name, but it wasn't Geistardt. His name was Hannes Gestert and he was an insignificant crook; not an SS officer but an unimportant corporal of Engineers.'

twenty

'It was vengeance,' Pel said. 'Plain, ordinary, common or garden vengeance. We caught the right murderer, but for committing the wrong murder.'

He paused and began to toy unenthusiastically with his little cigarette-rolling gadget. 'All the same,' he said, 'he'll pay the penalty. It was a pity for him Vallois-Dot got the wind up and wanted to give it all away.'

Darcy offered a Gauloise. Pel stared at it, then at the little gadget in his hands.

'Go on, Patron,' Darcy urged. 'Be a devil.'

Pel stared a moment longer, then he tossed the cigarette roller into the waste-paper basket and took a Gauloise. Lighting it, he blew out a cloud of smoke like the Riviera Express coming into the Gare de Lyon, and went on.

'They jumped to the conclusion,' he said, 'that because Gestert was a German and resembled Geistardt, that he *was* Geistardt. Especially when he showed himself interested in the woods at Bussy-la-Fontaine.' He drew a deep breath. 'However, we've also caught St Etienne's bank robbers and we've got the murderer of Madame Matajcek – at least, we have when he comes round. And finally, we found out who'd been robbing the chicken houses. The Chief's delighted about that, so it's not been a bad day's work.'

Darcy studied him. 'How did you fall on Massu, Patron?' he asked.

Pel rubbed his nose. 'I didn't,' he said. 'But when I saw his file, the whole lot came together. The meridional colouring, all the links to the Louhalle woman. He probably even looked like her. He was certainly sturdy like her, quick-tempered and free with his hands. That's why he wouldn't take me to see Madame Foing. He thought she might recognise his mother in him. Especially as I was going to see her about her.'

He paused, drawing at the Gauloise and coughing as if he were consumptive. 'When I saw his mother's name in his file, it hit me between the eyes.' He struck himself on the forehead with the flat of his hand. 'So I kept him busy writing a report while I got the Lab to examine his van. It had a slit in the tyre that matched the plaster cast Misset took, and they found traces of blood inside of the same group as Gestert's. And, of course, there were fingerprints all over it that matched the unidentified ones on Vallois-Dot's car and the car at Rivière-Française.'

'Was *he* after the swag from the de Mougy place, too, Patron?' Pel shook his head. 'I doubt if he was even interested.' He drew deeply on the cigarette. 'He was clever,' he went on. 'He was banking on the fact that, while we'd check every weapon we could find, we wouldn't check police weapons. Any more than we'd check police vehicles. And we didn't.'

'And Vallois-Dot?'

'He was going to throw himself on our mercy with the information that they'd got rid of a murderer of innocent Frenchmen. That was something that had burned in Massu's brain from the day he was old enough to understand. His mother was a heroine and the Germans had tortured her. No wonder he was always walloping old Bique à Poux. He thought *he* was a German, too.' Pel stubbed out the Gauloise and, while Darcy was absorbed in the story and unlikely to notice, hurriedly helped himself to another. 'It was the file,' he said again. 'The confirmation and the reason were there, in this building all the time. Father: Unknown. Mother: Dominique Louhalle. If he'd thought about it, he'd probably have stolen it. If *we'd* known, he might still have got away with it. His mother was known as a Resistance fighter and if his victim *had* been Geistardt – even if we'd *thought* his victim was Geistardt – his counsel could have pleaded provocation and the court might well have accepted it. Until he murdered Vallois-Dot, that is.'

Darcy frowned. 'But why did he never claim the Louhalle woman as his mother, Patron? Surely he could have been proud of her.'

'Could he? As a mother?' Pel shrugged. 'Perhaps he didn't fancy acknowledging the fact that she was a tart and he was the by-blow from a night's entertainment.'

'Poor bastard.' Darcy realised what he'd said and gave a twisted grin. 'And that little business in the wood?'

Pel shrugged. 'He was always too quick off the mark, and a policeman's gun's too handy. I was afraid if we tried to take him any other way he might start shooting. I'd also hoped,' he added slowly, 'that he might get himself shot and save himself from being dragged up in court by his friends and colleagues.'

Darcy sighed. 'While Geistardt, if he's still alive, is probably living in the lap of luxury in Argentina.'

'And the de Mougy plate,' Pel said in a flat voice, 'belongs to anyone with the patience to dig up one thousand hectares of Piot's land.'

MARK HEBDEN

DEATH SET TO MUSIC

The severely battered body of a murder victim turns up in provincial France and the sharp-tongued Chief Inspector Pel must use all his Gallic guile to understand the pile of clues building up around him, until a further murder and one small boy make the elusive truth all too apparent.

THE ERRANT KNIGHTS

Hector and Hetty Bartlelott go to Spain for a holiday, along with their nephew Alec and his wife Sibley. All is well under a Spanish sun until Hetty befriends a Spanish boy on the run from the police and passionate Spanish Anarchists. What follows is a hard-and-fast race across Spain, hot-tailed by the police and the anarchists, some light indulging in the Semana Santa festivities of Seville to throw off the pursuers, and a near miss in Toledo where the young Spanish fugitive is almost caught.

MARK HEBDEN

PEL AND THE BOMBERS

When five murders disturb his sleepy Burgundian city on Bastille night, Chief Inspector Evariste Clovis Désiré Pel has his work cut out for him. A terrorist group is at work and the President is due shortly on a State visit. Pel's problems with his tyrannical landlady must be put aside while he catches the criminals.

"...downbeat humour and some delightful dialogue."
Financial Times

PEL AND THE PARIS MOB

In his beloved Burgundy, Chief Inspector Pel finds himself incensed by interference from Paris, but it isn't the flocking descent of rival policemen that makes Pel's blood boil – crimes are being committed by violent gangs from Paris and Marseilles. Pel unravels the riddle of the robbery on the road to Dijon airport as well as the mysterious shootings in an iron foundry. If that weren't enough, the Chief Inspector must deal with the misadventures of the delightfully handsome Sergeant Misset and his red-haired lover.

"...written with downbeat humour and some delightful dialogue which leaven the violence." *Financial Times*

MARK HEBDEN

PEL AND THE PREDATORS

There has been a spate of sudden murders around Burgundy where Pel has just been promoted to Chief Inspector. The irascible policeman receives a letter bomb, and these combined events threaten to overturn Pel's plans to marry Mme Faivre-Perret. Can Pel keep his life, his love and his career by solving the murder mysteries? Can Pel stave off the predators?

'...impeccable French provincial ambience.' *The Times*

PEL UNDER PRESSURE

The irascible Chief Inspector Pel is hot on the trail of a crime syndicate in this fast-paced, gritty crime novel, following leads on the mysterious death of a student and the discovery of a corpse in the boot of a car. Pel uncovers a drug-smuggling ring within the walls of Burgundy's university, and more murders guide the Chief Inspector to Innsbruck where the mistress of a professor awaits him.

TITLES BY MARK HEBDEN AVAILABLE DIRECT
FROM HOUSE OF STRATUS

Quantity		£	$(US)	$(CAN)	€
	THE DARK SIDE OF THE ISLAND	6.99	11.50	15.99	11.50
	DEATH SET TO MUSIC	6.99	11.50	15.99	11.50
	THE ERRANT KNIGHTS	6.99	11.50	15.99	11.50
	EYE WITNESS	6.99	11.50	15.99	11.50
	A KILLER FOR THE CHAIRMAN	6.99	11.50	15.99	11.50
	LEAGUE OF EIGHTY NINE	6.99	11.50	15.99	11.50
	MASK OF VIOLENCE	6.99	11.50	15.99	11.50
	PEL AMONG THE PUEBLOS	6.99	11.50	15.99	11.50
	PEL AND THE TOUCH OF PITCH	6.99	11.50	15.99	11.50
	PEL AND THE BOMBERS	6.99	11.50	15.99	11.50
	PEL AND THE MISSING PERSONS	6.99	11.50	15.99	11.50
	PEL AND THE PARIS MOB	6.99	11.50	15.99	11.50
	PEL AND THE PARTY SPIRIT	6.99	11.50	15.99	11.50

ALL HOUSE OF STRATUS BOOKS ARE AVAILABLE FROM GOOD BOOKSHOPS
OR DIRECT FROM THE PUBLISHER:

Internet: www.houseofstratus.com including author interviews, reviews, features.

Email: sales@houseofstratus.com please quote author, title and credit card details.

TITLES BY MARK HEBDEN AVAILABLE DIRECT
FROM HOUSE OF STRATUS

Quantity	£	$(US)	$(CAN)	€
PEL AND THE PICTURE OF INNOCENCE	6.99	11.50	15.99	11.50
PEL AND THE PIRATES	6.99	11.50	15.99	11.50
PEL AND THE PREDATORS	6.99	11.50	15.99	11.50
PEL AND THE PROMISED LAND	6.99	11.50	15.99	11.50
PEL AND THE PROWLER	6.99	11.50	15.99	11.50
PEL AND THE SEPULCHRE JOB	6.99	11.50	15.99	11.50
PEL AND THE STAGHOUND	6.99	11.50	15.99	11.50
PEL IS PUZZLED	6.99	11.50	15.99	11.50
PEL UNDER PRESSURE	6.99	11.50	15.99	11.50
PORTRAIT IN A DUSTY FRAME	6.99	11.50	15.99	11.50
A PRIDE OF DOLPHINS	6.99	11.50	15.99	11.50
WHAT CHANGED CHARLEY FARTHING	6.99	11.50	15.99	11.50

ALL HOUSE OF STRATUS BOOKS ARE AVAILABLE FROM GOOD BOOKSHOPS
OR DIRECT FROM THE PUBLISHER:

Hotline: UK ONLY: 0800 169 1780, please quote author, title and credit card
details.
INTERNATIONAL: +44 (0) 20 7494 6400, please quote author, title,
and credit card details.

Send to: House of Stratus Sales Department
24c Old Burlington Street
London
W1X 1RL
UK

Please allow for postage costs charged per order plus an amount per book as set out in the tables below:

	£(Sterling)	$(US)	$(CAN)	€(Euros)
Cost per order				
UK	2.00	3.00	4.50	3.30
Europe	3.00	4.50	6.75	5.00
North America	3.00	4.50	6.75	5.00
Rest of World	3.00	4.50	6.75	5.00
Additional cost per book				
UK	0.50	0.75	1.15	0.85
Europe	1.00	1.50	2.30	1.70
North America	2.00	3.00	4.60	3.40
Rest of World	2.50	3.75	5.75	4.25

PLEASE SEND CHEQUE, POSTAL ORDER (STERLING ONLY), EUROCHEQUE, OR INTERNATIONAL MONEY ORDER (PLEASE CIRCLE METHOD OF PAYMENT YOU WISH TO USE)
MAKE PAYABLE TO: STRATUS HOLDINGS plc

Cost of book(s): —————————— Example: 3 x books at £6.99 each: £20.97

Cost of order: —————————— Example: £2.00 (Delivery to UK address)

Additional cost per book: —————— Example: 3 x £0.50: £1.50

Order total including postage: ———— Example: £24.47

Please tick currency you wish to use and add total amount of order:

☐ £ (Sterling)   ☐ $ (US)   ☐ $ (CAN)   ☐ € (EUROS)

VISA, MASTERCARD, SWITCH, AMEX, SOLO, JCB:

☐☐☐☐☐☐☐☐☐☐☐☐☐☐☐☐☐☐☐☐

Issue number (Switch only):

☐☐☐

Start Date: **Expiry Date:**

☐☐/☐☐   ☐☐/☐☐

Signature: ————————————

NAME: ————————————————————

ADDRESS: ——————————————————

——————————————————————

POSTCODE: —————————

Please allow 28 days for delivery.

Prices subject to change without notice.
Please tick box if you do not wish to receive any additional information. ☐

House of Stratus publishes many other titles in this genre; please check our website (**www.houseofstratus.com**) for more details.